HK Hollow
Dragoş Ilca
Proverse Hong Kong
2017

I0615896

Disclaimer

This is a work of fiction. Names, characters, businesses, organizations, places, events, and incidents are either the product of the author's imagination or are used fictitiously and only for fictitious purposes.

HK HOLLOW begins as a simple love story – love lost and love found – that records its bizarre elements in a matter-of-fact kind of way.

Carina and Guy are a young couple from Prague, studying in Amsterdam, who find themselves even more estranged when Guy leaves to spend a semester in Hong Kong. There, he meets Ling Fei-yan, a Chinese literature student. It doesn't take long for Guy to notice how much she reminds him of Carina – and to start liking her.

DRAGOȘ ILCA was born and raised in Romania. At nineteen, he left to study literature in Amsterdam. At twenty-two he became a teaching assistant at the Chinese University of Hong Kong, where he currently lives.

HK Hollow

Dragoş Ilca

Proverse Hong Kong

HK Hollow
by Dragoş Ilca
Alternate edition published in paperback in Hong Kong
by Proverse Hong Kong, April 2017.
ISBN: 978-988-8228-81-2
Copyright © Proverse Hong Kong April 2017.
Availability includes from
https://www.createspace.com/6985687

1st edition published in paperback in Hong Kong
by Proverse Hong Kong, April 2017.
ISBN: 978-988-8228-69-0
Copyright © Proverse Hong Kong April 2017.

Distribution and other enquiries to:
Proverse Hong Kong, P.O. Box 259, Tung Chung Post Office,
Tung Chung, Lantau Island, NT, Hong Kong SAR, China.
Email: proverse@netvigator.com;
Web: www.proversepublishing.com

The right of Dragoş Ilca to be identified as the author of this
work and of Jason S Polley to be identified as the author of
'Preface'
has been asserted by each of them
in accordance with the Copyright, Designs and Patents Act 1988.

British Library Cataloguing in Publication Data.
A catalogue record for this book is available
from the British Library.

PREFACE

A preface is "an introduction to a book, typically stating its [in this case, the specific case of Dragoş Ilca's *HK Hollow*, the novel's] "subject, scope, or aims." The etymology of "preface", a word synonymous in contemporaneity with "introduction", "foreword", "preamble", "prologue" and "prelude", among other less popular usages, has its origin in late Middle English, through Old French, by way of the Medieval Latin *praefatia*, which translates to "words spoken beforehand," from the verb *praefari*, meaning *prae* (before) + *fari* (speak).

The Oxford Dictionary of English (the very abridged *Oxford English Dictionary* that I keep on my desk; the 20-volume *OED* doesn't fit) definition I have provided in order to open—or preface—my preface to Ilca's *HK Hollow* presents a classic tautology. If "preface" is synonymous with "introduction", which, by the dictionary account presented above, preface indeed is, then the dictionary definition of "preface" amounts to "a preface to a book, typically stating its subject, scope, or aims." Also jumping out, for this preface-formulating reader at least, are the "or" and the plural "aims" following the Oxford comma in the definition of "preface." One might wonder why the "or" isn't an "and." Or an "and/or." Or why "subject" is singular" while "aims," for instance, is not. For that matter, why "typically"? Doesn't the ambiguous "or" make the "typically" more or less redundant? And how, anyway, can, or does, one "typically" "state" a book's "subject, scope, or aims"?

Another way to conceive of the last question above arises if we, meaning I, contemplate a specific "who" in lieu of an ambiguous "one." Who exactly writes, is writing, the "Preface"? And to what end? Let's phrase my inquiry differently: "typical" "words spoken beforehand" should lead to or "state" what preparatory conclusion? A, the, this preface is a "paratext," to use Gerard Genette's neologism. This is to say, the preface is a small text about the main text which is packaged in conjunction with the main text. Any text, in other words, is a (careful) conglomeration of paratexts all working in the service speaking to/about the main text. The preface—not unlike the blurbs and endorsements on the novel's back cover—complements and promotes the main text. The preface is "typically" read chronologically before the main text, if read at all, yet it is written following the completion, or the near-completion, of the main text. This much should be clear. This ostensible clarity, however, is actually more complicated than it *prima facie* appears.

What if the author, Dragoş Ilca himself, writes the preface to *HK Hollow*? Or what if Ilca decides to write the preface to *HK Hollow* under the guise of the male protagonist Guy? Or what if Ilca decides to write the preface to his novel under the guise of the book's indicatively (and/or maybe ironically?) named Guy, who himself writes under the façade of Carina, one of the novel's two female protagonists, this one the Czech girlfriend who remains in Amsterdam while Guy spends a semester studying abroad at the Chinese University of Hong Kong? Or what if Ilca, under the pretense of some fictional character, one who could in fact have a nonfictional name, writes a glowing paratext (or, just as effectively, a disparaging one; check out Banks' *The Wasp Factory* and Marcus' *Notable American Women*) to *HK Hollow* in order to drum up general interest in the main text itself? The possibilities for, and of, this and any prefatory paratext are manifold—which, one might wager, is why the very definition of "preface", or that featured in *The Oxford Dictionary of English* at least, appears to be, no, *is*, so equivocal.

What I've so far done here, and, yes, this is the third paragraph beginning with the word "what," is inadequately "introduce" the experimental *HK Hollow* by "stating its subject, scope, [and] aims." Ilca's erudite novel (which is his first, his first novel, I mean, not his first erudite novel, but it is his first erudite novel, albeit not the first erudite novel in a canon that includes other novels none of which is erudite) lapses into self-reflexivity on a number of occasions, such as in this sentence about the difficulty of representing the mutable nature of the self: "change passed by me as you finished reading this sentence." This postmodern sentence also plums the refined Proustian modern nature of memory and change. Is the subject merely static, simply "passed by," while transformation is the constant changing his surroundings? Who is this speaking subject, this "me"? Who is this interlocutor, this "you." And if, so Kafka forced us to interrogate in 'The Metamorphosis,' wherein the

Gregor Samsa who wakes up as a giant bug is still somehow the Gregor Samsa who went to sleep as an everyman, what is it that even defines the "me" as a "me" and the "you" as a "you"?

Is this "you" interlocutor Ling Fei-yan, the other female protagonist in the text, the symbolically unreadable *paramour* living in the female dorm below Guy, the woman who exotically (read: novelistically) haunts Guy's everyday western experiences of Hong Kong, in much the same way as both Fei-yan and Carina are hyperbolically (read: novelistically) haunted by Kafkaesque underworlds and surreal visions while separately travelling in Prague? Or is this "you" Carina, whose Amsterdam experiences, even after Guy's relocation to Hong Kong, weirdly continue to be omnisciently narrated by Guy himself? That is, of course, if we can believe in any solid sense of Guy's own "me." His name is Guy, after all. Perhaps he could be any "guy," any interchangeable "me," any person at all who is caught in the interstices of literature and life, of any "me" who limns the blurry borders between "fiction" and "nonfiction."

Or is it really Guy who narrates the unpunctuated (and sometimes cut-up *à la* Burroughs) Joycean internal monologues of Carina, two of which last for over three pages each? And if it is Guy, what might Dragoş Ilca thereby be proposing *vis-à-vis* the voice and agency of the other? Who speaks for whom? How? Indeed, can the other, "can the subaltern," so Gayatri Spivak has it, "speak" for herself at all? Can Guy even speak for Guy? We, we remember, are forced always already to remember, that he's a stranger, a *gweilo*, a "white ghost" in Hong Kong, in that strange land he can only ever see, only ever read, through western eyes.

Speaking of the modern Proust and Kafka, the high-modern Joyce, the existential Camus, the experimental Burroughs, and the erotic Kundera, Ilca's novel (which includes a number of bookshelves) also integrates postmodern pages of contemporary detritus in the form of text messages forming labyrinthine lists of replies that even vigilant readers can get lost within.

Or, given the changing, the evolving, passing us by, might "we" not already always be lost? In the case of *HK Hollow*'s hollows, we can't ever be sure if the "I," the "me," is, always is, or ever is, Guy's. Just as he's haunted by his love for literature and the *angoisse* of youth, Guy is haunted by the interloper "Hollowness." Similarly, Carina, who may just be Guy's or any guy's characterization of Carina as "Carina," is haunted by the *cafard* "Solitude." "Solitude" shadows her, even when she's not alone. Guy's relationship with "Hollowness" in the eponymous *HK Hollow* is the same: seemingly unshakeable.

In this at once street- and book-smart novel of ideas, each of the three main protagonists is lost. Each is alone. Each is followed. Each inhabits a world where the limits of realism expand and contract, where existential experience dissolves any easy distinction between fact and fiction, between manifested and manifesting, between literature and life. Read it. Get lost in it. And find your way out a better person for having done, or having attempted to do, so.

Jason S Polley
Associate professor,
ENG, HKBU

It was the shower that woke me, the water splashing down the tiles, and Carina's dreams of going to Hong Kong. Half a year is a long time and people can change their minds so fast. The water and uncertainty made her shudder. She squeezed the shampoo bottle twice, and let it work for ninety seconds before rinsing. Concentric circles over the scalp, rubbing with both hands five times at intervals of twelve seconds. I didn't get out of bed. Carina had all the bathroom to herself, and the noise of water against the tiles and curtain whistled that the train had left without me – it was better this way. Sneaking out of bed in the morning and taking showers alone had become a habit in recent days. Carina hoped I was smart enough to pick up on her hints. I was trying to get back to sleep. I couldn't notice her trying to tell me she was a morning person, I couldn't notice her getting out of our bed as soon as she got up, I couldn't notice her preference for a small but strong coffee. All I can say for myself is that I truly hated mornings, I had no wish to leave my bed right after I woke up, and I didn't like coffee. I couldn't be productive until evening, and I got better at doing work last-minute. Tea was good.

Seeing Carina's legs and just the bottom line of the towel wrapped around her walking towards the coffee machine, and then towards the closet was one of my morning pleasures. The shower was enough to wake me up, and whenever I heard her walking around the room I would squint my eyes and growl like a monster, tossing and turning in bed and trying to grab her arm, leg, or even reach under the towel to pull her back. But those legs avoided me every time, and they became better at carrying Carina away. Defeated, I would grab her pillow or gather the whole blanket around me and try to go back to sleep.

Everybody knows how hard it is to go back to sleep once somebody else is already up. When she closed the closet door it was like she slammed it after one of our fights. I could hear the wheels of the lingerie drawer running against the rails like I would hear my teeth grinding, and her sips from the coffee cup felt as if I was being sucked in, not the coffee. Carina's lips, pursing and making hundreds of tiny crevasses, her lungs expanding and pulling the coffee in, sending thousands of cold spikes in my skull. I bought her that cup from a Chinese store for our anniversary.

"Can't sleep?" she asked.

"Get back in here," I replied while lifting the blanket.

"No, I'm checking the things I need for Hong Kong."

"Why?"

"Why not?"

"I see."

"What about you? What are you doing?"

"I don't know."

"You have no idea, right?" she said, making the words more ironic than she intended.

"I don't know. I'll apply to a couple of places, and see what's gonna happen."

"Where do you want to go?"

"Berlin."

"That's it?"

"Maybe Hong Kong."

"But I'm going to Hong Kong."

"So?"

"Do you really want to compete with me?"

"Why not?"

"What if both of us get in?"

"I don't see anything wrong with that."

"I want to go someplace far away. Alone. My parents started saving money for it."

"I see."

"You're missing the point."

"Pretty sure I'm not."

I turned the other way and tried to go back to sleep. Carina pulled the curtains apart, drenching the room in light. The time was 8:45 and the sun would set at 21:11 with 14:52 hours of daylight.

I moaned. I hated beginning the day.

C arina took a moment away from sipping her coffee so she could watch me trying to get back to sleep. After 45 minutes of work, Carina allowed herself a five-minute break. Today was going to be a sunny day with temperatures up to 23 degrees Celsius and wind speed up to 25 km/h. Carina read that on the weather website, consulted every morning. The coffee woke her just enough to make out my profile details. Was it because of someone's eyes that you loved them the way she did? Because of their behaviour? Because they are handsome and/or wealthy? Or is it because I had hung around for so long that I became a given? Carina answered two-thirds negative and one third affirmative to the above questions. She wondered if that was how love should feel like after this much time, or if this was even love to begin with. In both cases, my approval rating was dropping from sixty-eight to forty-four percent.

Passion and youth are tangent functions. She never had such a relationship, out of her three official ones and five flings, where the function of her love had grown continuously towards stability. She wasn't sure she liked stability that much. Once you get serious about something, it loses its charm. Carina was not into getting bored. Boredom can be easily calculated. If a function is continuous, it's not hard to show that is monotonic. She remembered the days when she used to have fun, the nice days, the summer days, the laughing days she had spent with me, and she couldn't exactly pinpoint the day when the functions started to diverge: dishes piling up, assignments and exams multiplying, clothes that needed washing, or light bulbs that had to be changed.

But then she looked again at Guy who was struggling to fall asleep in her bed fifty minutes later. Of course, he was not the best. He didn't have a plan. He didn't think like a grown-up. He didn't know what to do with himself. Then again, Carina reasoned that the thing that kept the whole thing going was nothing more than *difference*. She knew I wasn't a morning person, she knew I didn't like coffee, and this became her only fun. Like sine and cosine. This whole difference, annoying at times, was a good remedy for boredom. Surely she would prefer something else, but at least you can't be bored once you're annoyed by most things, right? Carina smiled after the last remark. She was nothing like Guy, she was a fighter. And that is what you have to be in this man's world, when you're studying "manly" things like economics and mathematics. Also, Hong Kong is all about finances, numbers, percentages, and efficiency. Being a twenty-something young woman (and with more than three-quarters of her life spent before work and kids settled in), Carina couldn't figure out when she became a grown-up. She started talking about economic theories, politics, social issues in South Africa, governmental conspiracies, office outfits, and other things grown-ups talk about. She could make good use of the famous Chinese pragmatism and even teach me something about it, me who would starve in today's economy. Her résumé, emblazoned with the Hong Kong experience, would help secure a job in this time and place where nothing worked anymore, and she had to begin early for these kinds of things.

Her attention was again diverted towards Guy who had given up on sleeping and was staring at the ceiling. What was in his head? She looked around the room. It was a mess. Because both of them had been busy with their coursework, they didn't tidy up or do the dishes. Something moved in Carina's chest almost violently. She looked at Guy again. She was alright picturing me in such a mess. She sipped the last of her coffee, and before she could say anything, Guy pulled Carina into the bed and started kissing her neck. He threw the blanket over them. His dark hair like the legs of a spider touched her cheeks and mouth. Like always, Carina crossed her hand through Guy's hair, held his back, and looked up to the ceiling as he made his way down to her collar bone and the gap between her breasts. It had been a while since "no" didn't mean no, but it wasn't a total "no," because there he was, inside her, and she was outside him. She tried talking about it, but a relationship with someone like Guy turned into some sort of perverse duty. But he was simple and only looked for a quick fix. She could hear the guy jumping on the bed and taking her along, and if someone listened carefully, the springs on the bed went "Te-Reu! Te-Reu! Te-Reu!"

And there he was, Guy was pumping and pumping and pumping and thought he will never finish on Carina's flesh as it cringed sucking in his poison again and again and again. Guy feared his back might snap in two and Carina would suck him in whole and he was pumping and pumping and pumping, shoving himself into nothingness as both were dying, laughing the laugh that canceled teeth, lips, hairs, and rib cages.

It was done. Guy, finished, went to take a shower. Carina waited for him on the bed, counting the number of times she'd inhaled and exhaled: one, two, three, and four, short pause and then again, one, two, three, four… She had to change the bed sheets at some point today.

After the guy walked out of the bathroom, Carina took him by surprise:

"It's time to work. You should get dressed soon."

Guy replied almost automatically: "Yes, time to work."

Not love, just order and numbers.

Of all the cities she had traveled to so far, Ling Fei-yan found Prague the prettiest. It was the city of one of her favourite writers, Kafka. Fei-yan was inexplicably attracted to the old buildings, the bridges, and the Vltava. She took long strolls around the Old Town, in amazement along with the waves of tourists, and she took pictures of Charles Bridge – the guidebook said you need to "experience" it throughout the day. There was a string quartet that showed up around noon each day, which Fei-yan was particularly fond of. They used to stay until six in the evening, so every time after her lunch and those hypnotic walks, she would go up to the bridge and listen to them play. Fei-yan even filmed the quartet so that she could show her friends back home in Hong Kong. She also took some photos of the group – most likely for her wall of pictures with places she'd seen, places she hasn't been to yet, and her favourite lead singer, from an English band. She wasn't sure of it, but whenever the quartet noticed her taking pictures or filming, they played a particular song, and Fei-yan was pleased because she could recognize it. Although it made her smile (the musicians were secretly smiling as well), she didn't dare ask the musicians what the name of the song was. It was better this way – her memories of Prague would always be linked to that bridge, the song, and the string quartet. Some things are better left alone. She couldn't possibly have known the name of the song, but it was the first movement of Antonín Dvořák's *String Quartet No. 10 in E flat major Op. 51*. (She is not going to read this.) Fei-yan was excited and humbled one evening when the quartet was packing up their instruments – she would watch in amazement – and one of the members said to her in an Eastern European accent: "Don't film. Enjoy music now." He was right: How long had she concentrated on filming the quartet playing rather than let her sink into the music the way she did with the city?

After that evening, she did not see the quartet or hear her song; they must have found another bridge to play on. The next day Fei-yan waited for them to come and play like they used to. Of course, they didn't show up, but that gave her enough time to watch the people. The number of tourists steadily declined after two in the afternoon, leaving the night open to foreign couples and artists smoking their cigarettes by the edge of the water, all under the watchful eyes of King Charles IV. She laughed – King Charles must have seen as many people as China has now.

She searched for so long, but couldn't find Kafka's monument. It was clearly marked on the map, and she was standing right in front of the place where it was supposed to be. Thinking it was all just a hoax, not finding the statue she'd only seen pictures of on the internet was the sole regret of her trip. Fei-yan read the story related to the statue quite some time ago, and as a literature student herself, she really wanted to see how fiction looks in real life. When she finally saw Prague, she couldn't imagine how somebody as tormented as Kafka could have lived and worked in such a beautiful and sunny city.

While waiting for the monument to pop up all of a sudden, Fei-yan double-checked her map. Kafka was not there. When she lifted her nose from the map to ask somebody if the monument had been moved, the people around the monument were stripped naked and on top of their clothes almost like the statue Fei-yan was supposed to see. Tourists and locals – their eyes were white like a blind man's – walked around taking pictures of the old buildings, of themselves, and their food. Their bodies made up one of the most terrifying shows Fei-yan had ever seen: people crippled by skin defects, surgical scars, giant tumours, wrinkles. They didn't seem to notice that Fei-yan could see under their clothes. All those people and their deformed bodies were enjoying their last days in the streets of Prague. Lepers with fingers and ears and noses falling down in their soup, giant tumours almost translucent in the light of the sun, old people dancing in circles around a church, young people taking pictures of their backs to see if they had grown mushrooms, festered wounds and maggots inside the skin and cavities of people who had no idea what was going on. She ran to the hotel room, hid under the blankets of her bed, and didn't get out for the rest of the day. Fei-yan still had her clothes on. She never talked about this with anyone and decided it was best if she kept quiet. She was feeling sick from the heat, that was all.

Fei-yan wanted to see Europe, and for her, Prague was Europe. Of course, there are also old buildings, ancient structures, and even a wall in China that can be seen from outer space, but the thing she enjoyed most was the *difference*. This place looked different, the people were different, the buildings were sharp, pointed, and had crosses on top. They adorned the palaces and squares with statues that turned green in time. Their faces looked different, their languages were different, and they were eating and drinking differently (although it was very tasty). Fei-yan wanted to ride the same empty suit around the streets of Prague, like in Kafka's story, but in the end that was how she felt – like an empty pile of assorted clothes. Even so, Fei-yan didn't feel like going home. If anything, the world got smaller and smaller as she trekked around Europe. Her suit in the story may have been filled with air, but it kept going. She was in love with this distant land, and in her head, she pictured what life in Europe would be like with a young poet by her side. The scary daydream she had at Kafka's monument seemed so far removed from the Prague she saw...

Although she had trouble embracing Europe seen through her camera, Fei-yan admired the way Europeans dressed – particularly the guys. Tall, blond, dark-haired, blue-eyed, dark-eyed, light-blue shirts, skinny jeans, and brown oxfords, the Europeans didn't have trouble accepting her. Throughout her trip, she heard, "You're pretty," in at least two different languages. The French in Paris who were pointing at her saying, "*Tu es jolie!*" and laughing. The Germans who said, "*Sie ist schön,*" in the *Strassenbahn* and looked away. Fei-yan was happy to see she received attention from people in both continents. She had yet to discover how "You're pretty" sounded in Czech.

Fei-yan looked back at her wall filled with pictures from her trip to Europe. Now, back in Hong Kong, her wall had seen some more. For now, at least, the suit was drained, and she began living in-between some pictures she took some time ago of cities she might not visit a second time, and a strange episode at Kafka's monument.

There was no need for me to say the weather in Holland is horrible. After so much rain, and after so much wind, and after so many times getting soaked, you didn't care much. You tried to figure out ways of pedalling your bike faster to a cup of something hot. For this time of the year, Amsterdam was sunny. Whenever there was sun in Amsterdam, people did whatever they could to go outside and enjoy it while it lasted. After spending some time here myself, I did the same.

We didn't go out that day. We stayed in to clean the place. It didn't take too much time to adjust to the fact that once the sun is shining, you don't feel like doing anything. I shied away from doing things I didn't enjoy; after all, I was studying literature, and you either want to do it, or you find all the other subjects difficult. Me, I like reading books and people.

I was grumpy because I couldn't sleep and started looking out of the window or sticking my hand out to see how warm it was. I coughed a couple of times. Carina's dusting masked the tension building up. We didn't talk, but I was aware of her glances in my direction. She was always like that after we did it in the morning.

"Something wrong?" she asked.

"No, I didn't sleep so well."

"You shouldn't stay up late then."

"I'll try."

We made the bed and changed the sheets together. Afterwards, she went to take care of the dishes, leaving me with nothing to do. I insisted I should wash them, but she replied that if I had wanted to, I would have done them long before. I stayed behind her and the sink for a couple more minutes doing nothing. She kept on washing the dishes, ignoring me. She would always do that after we did it. A short period of opening followed by layers and layers of walls that sealed her away from me. I took a book from the book-case and started reading. I didn't want to read, so I stared out of the window, picturing flowers that could open and close in an instant.

"Guy?"

"Yes?"

"I might be going back to Prague," Carina said wiping a plate.

"Why?"

"With some student committee."

"That's nice. When?"

"Sometime in spring."

"But aren't you going to Hong Kong in spring?"

"I know, that's why I said 'might.'"

"Should be alright," I said trying to move past her sting.

"I don't like Prague," she interrupted me while arranging the plates in the cupboard.

"Why?"

"You know there are some people you just meet and don't like their faces?

"I guess."

"That's how I feel about it."

The dishes were done, the room was cleaned, and I had no idea when the sun went down. There was nothing else to do except read and go back to bed. Time was running out of patience. I wondered if Carina felt about Amsterdam the way she did about Prague. We rarely left our room. I liked watching Carina's legs as she changed her clothes and I could hardly keep myself from grabbing them, but both of us knew where that was going.

I accepted that one of us was going to leave after I saw Carina printing out the documents for going abroad. It was one of those dreams you could barely remember in the morning, and in the dream Carina or myself opened the door to the room and was greeted by Solitude itself. I guess people who are condemned to be lonely are the same, just like pilgrims.

It's hard to give up on something you've grown accustomed to, no matter how bad it was. Carina and I knew things were going to change, no matter who was leaving and where, but we were too afraid to say it. When we tried, we always ended up fighting.

Traveling changes people. We *want* to fall in love with distant places and exotic men and women, tell stories of our journeys, and the will to sacrifice a lot to satisfy a fraction of our hidden desires, just to preserve even a shallow memory like a photo or a souvenir. And that was where Carina and I tried to get to. We weren't aware of it, but something outside us drove us to it. We *wanted* to go, we *wanted* to be torn apart the same way we shared something painful. We wanted to make Solitude happy.

Imagination was the only thing that helped me fill the gap between us. Things won't be the same after the pilgrimage.

In most cases, it was easier to destroy something than improve it. It was unbearable to think about loneliness, about taking back your share of the world, your half of the room, about sleeping next to Solitude.

"What are you thinking about?" Carina said after she caught me staring at the window.

"Nothing."

We stopped talking. She got back to work, although her angry glances pointed to something else. All that thinking meant that I was up to no good.

Carina's preparations for going abroad were too perfect. Her too-powerful excitement, her desire to break with everything, and all her talking about Hong Kong with a joy that betrayed arrogance, tired me. She begged some outside force to destroy her plans – just to see from a safe distance how frustration and anger and resentment were struggling in a web.

“Are you done? The deadline is today.”
“Yes.”
“Where?”
“Berlin.”
“And?”
“And that's it.”
“Are you happy now?”
“Don't worry. I'll see after I've got in.”
The deadline was in three hours and if I hurried, I could send out another application for Hong Kong. Carina always said it would be a shame not to take advantage of an opportunity if it's there.

I said I had some work to do, so she left me alone. I took the statements and the forms I had already filled in for Berlin, and gave them a twist. Changing bits and pieces the whole thing was done with three minutes to spare.

“Are you finished?”
“Yes.”
“What did you have to write?” Carina asked.
“Another application.”
“Really? Where?”
“Hong Kong.”
“Seriously?”
“Yes.”
Her face was expressionless. She muttered something about visiting our neighbour and left. I tried coming closer to the bed, explaining I also have a choice, maybe even to try to comfort Carina somehow. Like always, she twitched in a way that was barely noticeable whenever she didn't want to be touched. Carina left and I sat in the armchair opening a book.

At her friend's place, Carina was so upset she didn't even want to drink her tea. You didn't even like tea, did you Carina? She clenched her fists and bit her lip.

“How could he do that? He won't leave me alone!”
“It's fine, don't worry. I'm sure you'll work something out.”
“No, we won't.”
“So why don't you break up with him?”
“I can't.”
“Why?”
“He wants me to be unhappy.”

"What are you talking about? Just because you want to go there, that doesn't mean he has no right to apply."

"Of all the places in the world, why Hong Kong? I want to go there!"

"How should I know?"

"I don't know what's in his head. He just sits in his armchair, reads all day, and writes his papers and articles. He barely talks about anything. We only do it because we have to. He just stares out of that stupid window. And I tell him everything. Everything! He knows how much I want to go abroad, and he does this, the son of a bitch!"

"Try to talk about it."

"I can't. I don't feel like it. He never tells me about his plans, I just think he himself doesn't know what he wants. He's always been like that, and it drives me crazy. I *hate* this about him. And I tell him everything!"

"Why are you telling me all this? Go talk to him."

"Thanks for the help."   ******

In my head, Hong Kong and Berlin were mixed up: the Brandenburg Gate was on top of some skyscrapers, Bruce Lee's statue on the Avenue of Stars was in the middle of Alexanderplatz, the octopus on top of the Sony Centre was covering the entire skyline of Hong Kong, old blond Germans were practicing tai chi in the Tiergarten, dim sum places were sharing the space with Turkish kebab shops, and a bunch of fat Asians dressed like Bavarians drank huge beers in a biergarten nearby. This dream, more like a stroboscopic sequence of images, I had in the armchair waiting for Carina. Walking around the incest of Berlin-Hong-Kong or Hong-Kong-Berlin, walking the streets behind the Brandenburg Gate, the rows of trees were replaced with Bank of China after Bank of China, and their lights flickered at the same time, everything in the world going at a metronomic pace. A bunch of Chinese schoolgirls came out of a Soviet tank, giggling and pointing at me.

At the end of the road, the Statue of Victory was waiting. Made out of solid gold on top of a huge column, the statue had been replaced by the most beautiful woman I had ever seen. A bit shorter than I was, long, straight hair, round face (but not too round), her wings were not too big.

Looking straight up at the base of the column on which the Statue of Victory rested, I knew what I had to do. I climbed towards the top like a professional. The Chinese schoolgirls behind me all took their old Leica cameras out and started taking pictures. As I reached the top, the woman's wings fluttered for a second as if she was trying to get away, but as soon as I embraced her, the layer of gold that covered her melted. Her eyes became darker than any shade of black I'd like to wear. She dropped her spear and her crown of laurel. Right there, on top of the column, watching the light show play on the Bank of China buildings, under the Chinese schoolgirls' pictures, we did it. The flash from the cameras was so powerful it made me uncomfortable. I was being watched having sex. Doesn't it take a kind of courage to have sex while someone is filming or taking pictures? The angel tried to cover me with her wings, away from the M-lenses of the Chinese schoolgirls. The pigeon on the statue's head was restless and flew away. When both of us were almost there, music started. It was a victory march. ******

Twice that week Carina watched me sleep. I didn't usually go to sleep so early. She looked at me resting the book in my lap, my head tilted on the side, breathing regularly. On her way back, she practiced her twenty-one lines: how to start the conversation, how to approach me so that we don't fight, what are my plans, and why did I go for the same city she did? But all her thoughts, like her anger, melted away once she saw me sleeping in the armchair. Carina smiled. She came close to me and started stroking my hair.

"You fell asleep like an old man. Let's get you to bed."

She helped me take my shirt off and put on my pajamas. Once I stood up, I covered my shame the best I could. She had something to say to me, but for now, I was resting on her breast. Once Carina was sure I was asleep, she went to the bathroom and washed her hands three times, thirty seconds each time, with a balanced pH soap.

It took me a while to figure it out. *"I am pleased to inform you that your application was found to be a strong one and you have officially been nominated to participate in the bilateral exchange programme to Hong Kong."* Ten minutes later, I received a text from Carina. She wasn't that lucky. Now it was even worse. We all knew how much Carina wanted to go to Hong Kong and maybe that's why she was so mad. Not going abroad must have been bad enough, but me on top of that? Walking to our place, I could picture both of us building the wall that would be larger than all walls, walls so heavy that they would seal us off forever. Battalions of soldiers, pillboxes, and tanks parading in front of each other, civilians building bunkers and machine-gun nests just in case. We rushed to get our weapons, making the people paranoid. Who was going to press the button first? There were things I had to face before I left. For now, I laughed at the whole thing. A sick laugh like you would utter the moment before Little Boy hit the ground.

She was sobbing in our room, on our bed. The curtains were drawn. It smelled like Solitude.

"I'm sorry."

"You shouldn't see me like this."

"I've seen worse."

Pause.

"It's not that important. If you go or not, it's not such a big change."

"But I wanted to go so much!" Crying.

"I'm sorry."

"What are you so sorry about? Did you get your results back?"

"Yes, we all did."

"And?"

I didn't reply.

"And?"

More silence.

"And?" she said.

I looked at the window. A bird was resting on the sill. It flew away after a while. I felt like laughing again.

"I'm in."

"Where?"

"Both."

Your rigid face, Carina.

"Are you sure?"

"Yes, the e-mail came in this morning," I said really fast.

"Are you going to go?"

"I'm not sure."

We stood like that for a while. We were a pair of statues looking into each other's souls. Who was going to press the button first? Who would start the mutual assured destruction? I had to hold back my laughter. Maybe Carina was hoping for the same thing, for me to start laughing and say it was all a hoax like all the other ones I pulled. But the laughter didn't come, just a blank stare and twitches on a big red button.

"Did you read *The Little Prince*?"

Your ashen hair, Carina.

"Really? Is this the best you can do?"

"Did you?"

"Yes, a while ago."

"Remember the thing with the sheep eating the flowers with thorns?"

"Yes."

"What are the thorns good for?"

"Nothing. The sheep eats the flower anyway."

"You're just like that flower."

Carina had a strong impulse to hurt me, strangle me, slap me, run to get the kitchen knife and cut me 1001 times, throw herself out of the window. Carina couldn't understand life. She was too much a grown-up for that. Carina hated my luck more than *The Little Prince*. She hated herself, too. She hated us. Carina couldn't understand life. Why can't you understand life, Carina, aren't you a grown-up?

"You're going to Hong Kong," she muttered. "Congratulations."

"Don't start hating me, I haven't gone there yet."

"I can't believe the work I did, and then in you come, and you're going to Hong Kong. I hope you have the time of your life. In Hong Kong!" More crying.

"You don't want me to go?"

"No."

"Remember the flower? The thorns?"

"Fuck you."

Pause.

"I feel like killing myself," she said with an affected smile. "I'm going to tell my family you're going to Hong Kong, and I'm not and then they won't give me money to study in Amsterdam and they'll say I'm good for nothing and make me work at the grocery store in Prague where your little sister comes and does the groceries, and type in numbers all day. 9.99, 24.99, pay for five and get one beer free! I can give you change, sure!"

More crying. Slammed doors.

The armies were gathering, the walls getting higher. Somewhere, on a distant planet, a sheep was eating a flower with thorns and both of them were okay with it.

Carina blamed herself for not speaking to Guy next to her in bed. The electronic clock showed 0:05. She didn't know what went wrong, but at this point, she didn't have any thorns so her tears were for nothing. All Carina could hope for was that there would be a mistake in the system, that Guy somehow would go through this miracle, or that the plane would blow up on its way there. On a distant planet, a sheep opened its mouth leaning down towards the ground.

Carina could only blame herself. Why did she leave this threat looming above her, above us? When did she and Guy start behaving as if we were in the Cold War? All her gestures, all her small separatist statements turned into a routine, and yet, nobody could talk about it. All she knew now was that she had an army stationed in front of some giant walls that could attack at any moment.

Solitude crept in through the window. You remembered Solitude, didn't you, Carina? It took some time, but it found you again. You couldn't escape Solitude, Carina. There was no doubt; this was the room it was supposed to be in. Solitude crawled across the walls and then along the ceiling, trying not to wake them up. Solitude was watching over Carina. The rose with the useless thorns, Carina. Out came a hand from Solitude's ragged clothes. Sheep weren't the only thing you needed to watch out for, Carina. There were other things eating roses. Roses could also be eaten from the inside, Carina. Solitude had a worm in its hand and placed it on Carina's cheek. The worm made its way to Carina's ear and in it went. Solitude was singing a lullaby that only Carina could hear. Just like when you were a child, Carina.

The worm inside her brain was moving. Worms can grow like that, Carina, you can sing to them. Just like the roses in your mother's garden, Carina. The worm started on Carina's likes, frustrations and theories like the most thorough librarian totalling up to 471. The worm was chewing her thoughts, thoughts that had no logical explanation. She checked off every single item on the checklist, and Guy sleeping next to her in the pitch black room would go to Hong Kong. Carina hated Guy's peaceful sleep and the desire to hurt him grew as fast as the worm inside her brain. *"It's easy, right? Just hurt him! Put the pillow over his face. Do it!"* She tried to silence the voice like in a bad dream, but the worm spoke even louder. *"After he leaves, it's only you and me! He's already dead. Look again!"* Carina lifted her head off the pillow and in the darkness of the room she could still make out Guy's face. It was eaten by maggots. She barely held in the crying. The guy moaned and turned over to the other side. Carina calmed herself by saying she just had a bad dream. On the clock, eight more minutes passed. *"Just you and me, love."*

No matter how much she'd hurt the guy next to her, he was still leaving. Maybe if she showed him what he was missing, then maybe she would have a chance of getting revenge.

But then her thoughts changed. If Guy next to her is going to leave, what is going to happen to her? For the first time in months, Carina was scared about what was going to come. We were alone in Amsterdam, there were hardly any other people who could speak the language we did, and we hardly had any friends. We were <u>alone</u>. The worm inside her brain coiled. Solitude didn't talk very much, Carina, it just stood there and watched. You can talk to the worm, Carina, he is a nice conversation partner.

She was uncomfortable. Her breathing picked up, and her heart felt strange, as if it wanted to break free from her chest. She was going to be alone. Hearing her, the guy next to Carina woke up and halfheartedly asked, "You okay?" She turned the other way but there was no way for Guy to see the red contour of her eyes. Barely moving her lips, Carina could only say, "Yes." Solitude crawled to the corner of the room and waited. Solitude liked to wait, Carina.

It was hard to tell whether Carina found some serenity in the following weeks or if she let her worm grow. Her rage, her insecurities, her family scolding her over Skype for not going abroad finally cooled off. We could talk about my departure without having to cry or insult each other. We made a list and we bought some things I could use. Carina wanted to help me get some new clothes, shoes, even underwear. It was her self-imposed moral duty to have me well-dressed before I left. She calculated we spent around 120 euros.

Carina started making plans to keep herself busy. "Time goes by so easily when you're doing your homework," she said. When I'm back from my odyssey (that's how she called it), we'll go on an adventure, just the two of us. A lot of catching up to do.

The thing that made me suspicious of Carina in the first place was her evasiveness whenever it came to Hong Kong. Being quiet about a sensitive issue is often a bad omen, like a rival superpower devising new weapons. The way I lied to myself, I finally hoped Carina had come to her senses and made peace with my pilgrimage. The way she handled her defeat had a normal trajectory: denial, anger, acceptance, and then everything fizzled out in depression. We were coming out of the acceptance phase. Carina told me her mom and grandma believed in destiny, and her destiny was not to go to Hong Kong. You can't change your destiny, she said. I did it in three hours.

In our last week, she was nicer than usual. That made me question things again, as if she wanted to show me a glimpse of what I was going to miss. Carina cooked for me, we went out on a couple of dates in some nice restaurants around Amsterdam and had sex once we got back, went shopping a couple of times, and I woke up early to get her coffee. We listened to Johnny Cash's cover of "Hurt" while hugging almost naked in bed. Carina counted the times we listened to the song and it was around eighty-eight. She wanted to make my fantasies come alive and one day Carina dressed up as a schoolgirl (I always had a thing for schoolgirls) one night. She bought the outfit somewhere around the Red Light District in Amsterdam. She hated going there. But even then with Carina dressed up like the obedient student she was, neither of us were there. We showered separately and I untangled her pony tail after everything was over. Nobody could say we didn't give it a try.

The day had come when Carina had to go back home for the winter holidays. I was leaving a couple of days after New Year's Eve. On the train to the airport, Amsterdam was beginning to wake up. There were ferries on the IJ as the train slowly pulled into Amsterdam's Central Station. Outside, people were biking to work or doing the groceries and the old buildings looked even older in the gray light so common for Amsterdam. Few passengers exited the train; even fewer entered from the platform. Next to me, next to all her luggage, Carina struggled not to cry and tried to squeeze a smile every time she looked at me. We barely spoke during the train ride but our hands were touching each other like a hint. Neither of us tried to hold on tight.

We both stopped outside her gate. Carina took a quick look at her wristwatch. It was 10:26. That was it, the moment we'd been waiting for but had been too afraid to talk about. The moment when our stories would no longer come together. I remember we said boring things, like "I'll miss you very much," or "I'll skype you every chance I get," or "Take care in Hong Kong," and "Say 'hi' to your family for me."

Carina held her breath for our last kiss. Because we woke up late, we didn't have time to brush our teeth, and morning breath was one of the most disgusting things in Carina's world. Once we opened our eyes, I could see she was repulsed but she struggled not to show it. She smiled, and left. Her eyes became wet the instant she turned away for the check-in. The experience was almost violent. I wanted to say something nice, something inspiring, even something heroic. All I could do was stay there and watch. Some things are better left unsought for.

Hong Kong seemed so far away. Watching Carina for a moment after I could no longer see her, I couldn't picture myself in a place so far away. My imagination was the only thing between Amsterdam and the "Fragrant Harbour." ******

"It's just you and me now."

Ling didn't adjust her sleeping pattern after her trip to Europe just yet. Once she landed in Hong Kong, the place seemed desolate. School was almost starting, and Fei-yan found herself pasting photographs of herself and her favourite bridge in Prague on the wall. The view from her room alienated her even more, like a twisted primitivism. From the ninth floor she could see the sun creeping up behind the mountain, turning the water purple. The ferries were aligning themselves in their piers, and just behind the tree line separating the highway, people were lining up for soccer practice. In the neighbourhood across the water, Ma On Shan, in the apartment towers, the lights went off one by one. Trains carried people to their work, and Fei-yan found it funny to correlate the number of lights turning off with the trains passing by.

Going to bed early in the morning became Fei-yan's habit. But today, she was determined not to sleep in because she heard about the exchange students' visit to the art studios. They were already here, and she hadn't met all of them.

With only a couple of minutes to spare, since she overslept (some promises you just can't keep), Fei-yan threw some clothes on and rushed to meet the other people for the studios tour. She called one of her colleagues to see where they would meet up. What if she didn't have that number in her phonebook? She would have missed the trip. Fei-yan took the train one stop, and when she got there, she was disappointed to see the group was not as big as she thought: three foreigners and four Chinese girls. One of them was apparently acquainted with the organizer – he was enrolled in his literature class. Asked by another to give his last name, Guy answered: "Why would I wanna do that?" His remark raised some eyebrows, and Fei-yan concluded he had poor social skills. Still, when they were introduced by the organizer, Fei-yan smiled and shook his hand. The guy repeated her name a couple of times, just to get the pronunciation straight. Fei-yan. Fēi-yān. Fei-yan. She found that disturbing but being polite never hurt anybody. Off they went.

From the subway station, the group had to walk for fifteen minutes. The studios were in an old factory complex and they were only open for a couple of days every year. The whole concept intrigued Fei-yan because she missed it last year. It was something very attractive – forbidden almost – to see the place where artists work. There was also something strange about the foreigner she just met. Although Fei-yan concluded he had poor social skills, she wanted to give him another chance. Since all the other people were talking to each other, Fei-yan approached him once more. She learned he was studying literature in Amsterdam, and had got here a week or so ago. Immediately finding some common ground, Fei-yan said she was also doing literature, and they started talking about books. The guy's answers were strange, as if he were trying to sabotage himself. Fei-yan asked if he had any favourite authors, and then the guy opened some serious philosophical problems all of a sudden: How can you have a "favourite" author? What are the things that make him "favourite?" Is it about the things he writes about? Is it the style? Is it the message? Taken by surprise, Fei-yan didn't know what to reply and was happy that her conclusion wasn't wrong.

Then, he replied he doesn't have *one* favourite author. He liked a particular aspect or theme or twist of phrase in a writer, but he never placed one on top of the other. His answer was unconventional, but Fei-yan was getting through.

After a while, the guy asked if she wrote, and then it was his turn to think the girl next to him was strange. Fei-yan answered: She did some riding in her time, but nothing too serious. She didn't even use a helmet. The guy nodded and then went silent. What was wrong with everybody? Since he got here, he didn't manage to have a decent conversation with any of these people.

Excusing himself for maybe talking too fast, Guy said he was referring to "writing," not "riding," and then he held an invisible pen in his hand, wiggling it in the air. Now it was Fei-yan's turn to feel embarrassed, and then she quickly replied she tried writing – all literature people do. Part ironic, part arrogant, the guy smiled.

The visitors received maps of the rooms that were part of the tour, after they arrived. They found themselves mingling with other workers carrying around heavy carts of materials in big elevators that had noisy grills and metal doors that were very hard to open and close.

The halls were old and dusty. The air was stale. Chunks of concrete were missing from the floor and the walls, revealing the insides of the building. Electric cables, pipes, debris, and workers – Fei-yan thought there was some kind of mistake, that the group had got off at the wrong level, or that they were in the wrong place. The workers who passed by were not very friendly. Once they stepped inside one of the studios, they were stepping in different worlds. The flooring was changed, the setting was changed, the lighting was changed, the statues, the pictures, the walls were changed. With every room the group visited, they could either witness the weirdest or "artistic" settings. A black and white rendering of a house pulverized by the blast of an atomic bomb, shadow sculptures, a pitch-black room with a box inside, a tent hung up from the ceiling, wooden skulls and geometric metal sculptures and close-ups of mouths holding their breath as long as they could on TV recordings – uncanny and beautiful at the same time. Once the group stepped out on the hallways they were reminded that they were in a dusty and decrepit factory. But once they stepped inside a studio, everything was transformed. The group was carried into different faces of the building, like you would read a story in different ways. Fei-yan believed the almost-disabled factory was a long-extinct animal that died a slow and painful death and the group was walking around its skeleton and cavities. The workers were the maggots and bacteria that turned it into fuel. The studios, the enchanted worlds, they were the mosses and mushrooms that grew on its body. Fei-yan sat and watched in amazement. For her, this trip inside the factory was just like roaming the streets of Prague.

The group separated and Fei-yan often found herself next to the guy from Amsterdam. They weren't talking that much, but they did look at each other. The guy often came to her and pointed things out. Fei-yan saw the guy was troubled by something. She sought him out in another room and said she didn't understand either. Relieved, the guy smiled. In the beginning, though, the guy was annoyed by how Fei-yan went into the same rooms as he did and teased her, but in the end, they began a secret chase throughout the factory like fifth-graders.

The other parts of the group left earlier, which made her, Guy, and the organizer the only three people who had seen all the studios. They took the train back to the campus, talking about the things they'd seen. The organizer went a different way after they got out, leaving Fei-yan alone with the guy to walk back to their rooms. Having nothing better to do, she suggested having a drink somewhere. The guy smiled.

At the café, Fei-yan asked the guy if he wrote. "Hmm, not really, only a couple of short stories, but they're so bad. I don't think I have them anymore. I don't even remember their plots. Of course, they were terrible. But when I did it, when I sat at my computer and started typing, it was just like today – stepping into *something else*. It felt like discovering masturbation all over again."

The guy sitting across the table was either a lunatic or one of the smartest people she'd ever met. It embarrassed her. After a moment of silence, when she chased away unbecoming images with Guy's hands in his pants thumping the underside of the table, she asked him what was the last thing he wrote a paper about. The guy said he did some work on *Cloud Atlas* and compared the novel with the movie. He then went on for ten minutes talking about how he didn't like the book, and yet it was so "juicy" from an academic perspective, all the while the image of Guy bent over and thumping the table came back to her.

They had to cut their conversation short – Fei-yan got a phone call and talked in Chinese. It sounded important. Despite the guy's obvious poor social skills, she said she had a good time and wanted to talk to him again. The guy stared out of the window and finished his coffee.

C arina opened the door. Solitude was waiting. The embrace, colder than the room she just stepped into, made her drop all her luggage and cry. The room temperature dropped to 18 degrees Celsius.

She started feeling dizzy from all the crying, and looked around the place. The desolation, almost palpable, gave her an arousing finality. All life ended the moment she stepped inside. The worm inside her brain, patiently growing over the winter holidays, patiently growing and shadowing blunt conversations with long-lost relatives and half-forgotten friends over Christmas dinner, coiled even more. Carina could swear she heard him telling her, "*I told you this was gonna happen!*" The whisper, slithering through Carina's Eustachian tube a length of thirty-five millimeters, swimming in her membranous labyrinth, finishing at her auditory nerve twenty-five millimeters away, spoke to her at the centre of what it meant to be herself. "*He left you, he's not coming back, look at the mess in your room, he didn't even bother to tidy it up, you're going to stay here and he won't like you anymore!*"

Carina couldn't bear to listen. In a corner of the room, Solitude stood and watched the whole scene. From time to time, it would breathe out the cold. "*You're on your own now. There is no one here left for you. He made a fool out of you, he's in Hong Kong now, he's having the time of his life, he's fucking all those Chinese girls and you're sitting here crying like the worthless piece of shit you are!*"

Carina was crushed. She grabbed her breasts and squeezed as hard as she could. She wanted to answer the worm but she needed air. She walked to the window, pulled the curtains away, and opened them as wide as she could. How easy it would have been to just lean a bit more forward! "*Do it!*" the worm whispered. "*Do it!*" he said in a louder voice. "*Do it! It's the only way you're going to hurt him! He's not going to remember you, he's fucking Chinese girls! Dooooooooooooo iiiiiiiiiiiiiiiiiiiiiiiiitttttttttttttttttttttttt, he'll never forget you!*"

Carina stood for a moment and looked out of the window. The rain made the hairs on her arms rise. From its corner, Solitude was watching the struggle. Carina wanted to speak. The other rooms across the block were looking like empty, dusty drawers. Still by the window, she turned away and looked at the whole mess.

The worm grew so big, it had to squeeze itself inside her convolutions. One by one, all of Carina's optic nerves, larynx, pancreas, ovaries, pulmonary alveoli, smooth, striated, and cardiac muscles, bladder and intestines were under the control of the worm.

Speak now, if you can.

Jbcbachbbcea
vvshclacada;'l[pl.
jbnbgb

You're not trying hard enough.

Ncajcnabdcbeyacan'ttalknowjan
static noise
cdbcahdbwuh127e1@$^&P:M:

Come on. We're almost there.

He left you.

Ancjeahyeshedidleaevhbhaebceacacad

You hate him. You hate him with all your heart. THE COWARD! HE LEFT YOU ALONE HERE! HE LEFT YOU HERE WITH ME! WE'RE GONNA PARTY LIKE ROCKSTARS!

UyhwahbHELEFTMEHELEFTMEHELEFTME!@&$!NO NONONONONONONO

TELL-HIM-YOU-HATE-HIM! HE'S AT THE AIRPORT NOW! TEXT-HIM-AT-THE-AIRPORT

ihatehim! Ihatehim! ihatehim! pickinuphisbag!

COWARD! HE-HATED-YOU! HE-COULDn'T-STAND-

YOU!
HE's-SO-HAPPY-NOW! He'S GONE!

COWARD!COWARD!COWARD!HAPPY!HAPPY!HAPPY!T
EXT!TEXT!TEXT

Solitude crept away from Carina's head. It grinned. Its tail twirled with satisfaction.

Carina piled up the few things I had left in her room and threw them on the unkempt bed. She made sure to put my favourite books on top. After, she pulled the curtain back. The room was dark again. She arranged one of my t-shirts and pair of pants on the armchair, and stripped herself. The way she pulled her panties just for a bit and the alternate hip movement, watching the turquoise underwear I'd bought for her slide down her waxed legs made her giggle. Then, Carina jumped onto the mattress, one hand squeezing the edge of the bed and one hand under her belly. She was amazed at how big it got. Solitude smiled. It crept away from the bureau in the corner, crawled on the ceiling and landed next to Carina. Solitude didn't speak to Carina, it just acted, that's what you had the worm for. A hand appeared from the ragged clothes. Smiling, Solitude touched her strip of pubic hair and she was finished in under thirty seconds. Carina's nipples were hard from the cold.

The worm inside her head relaxed for a short while. In bed together, Carina squeezed Solitude in her arms. There was a small space between the curtain and the window and 4 drops of water fell inside. Carina was worried – maybe someone heard her scream. Calming down her breath, she put some clothes on and wrapped herself in Solitude's rags. Solitude licked her ear. The long trip back to Amsterdam had worn her down.

I've only been here for a couple of days and I already feel overwhelmed. The flight to Hong Kong was a test of endurance on its own. The airplane, lifting me 1,000, 2,000, 5,000, 10,000 metres in the sky uprooted me, and at the same time, the tin can, heavier than air, made me unbearably light. I was no-one's.

I finally had time to think about the things I did yesterday. I disliked going to orientation weeks, registrations, unpacking, learning my way around the place, and meeting new people from across the globe. My life these past days had been like that of an ascetic, but I didn't know what to make of it. I received several texts from Carina, telling me how bad she felt and how much she hated me for leaving her. I had hoped the crushing guilt would leave me soon. Busy, hardly any time for me to think about what I'd done, about how I'd stolen another person's dream of going abroad. Carina's delusion was even greater because *I* went. If it was anyone else, then it would have been alright, but *me* leaving – that was so much closer to the heart.

Awkward, frightened, confused, those were my first few days here. The city, the skyscrapers, felt unnatural, and at the back of my head I thought, how can one build such a monster of a city? From down there, the buildings were so tall that they were a technical drawing on the arch of the sky. The lightness I had during the plane ride whispered I'm too far away from everything and I shouldn't care about what's happening to a girl 9,000 kilometers away. Isn't running away from things what I always wanted?

Walking around Mong Kok at night, you'd get a tidal wave of stimuli from all directions. Everything seemed threatening: cars and buses accelerating past traffic lights, giant advertisements I couldn't read, old women sticking massage parlour flyers in my face. I realized I knew nothing about this place, and the only way to talk was in a language that was not mine. In a metro station, those faces in the crowd, the lights and characters I couldn't understand, the smelly tofu, the unbreathable air filled me with anxiety and paranoia. The way I was blinking, the way I was interrupting the flow of artificial light filtered my walk in such a way that it looked like a damaged film.

People. I had never seen so many people. The lights of the city washed everything in noise. Languages I could not understand, strange-looking people, each with a story to tell. I could only imagine writing about such people, book after book, creating intricate layers and added complexities, and then the stories would generate other ones and so on. The potential of filling Hong Kong with its own stories was endless.

Stepping into such worlds you can't understand was about the language. Cantonese, an up-and-down sounding language, panicked me. The frustration of not understanding what is being said to you or what everyone is saying or advertising comes from a pervasive need to bend everything to your own will. And there I was, the Westerner marching in and condemning and complaining about a language I could not speak.

The crowd was me, and I was the crowd. Individuality didn't matter at this point. You could only relate yourself to the people you were walking next to. To my left, to my right, forward and backwards, I shared a deranged sense of intimacy with the people next to me. I could peer onto their phones, onto their Facebook and Whatsapp conversations, I could notice their skin defects, I could see the dandruff on their shoulders, and yet they were strangers to me, stepping into worlds I could not tap into. In itself, the act of walking was done in a very ordinary manner, and one would soon develop skills that reduced your personal space, and yet still not touching or rubbing against each other. You couldn't escape the crowd, the fleshy prison of Mong Kok. I was never so hollow.

Trying to find a way out of the crowd, I looked up. The city lights were bright enough to cause epileptic seizures, but they distracted from the crappy apartment buildings and the poor people who lived in them. Most likely, the tenants and landlords above owned or worked the shops below for sixteen hours a day and knew nothing else. I thought that was exactly how my relationship worked and it made me smile. In Amsterdam, you couldn't see them because of the gray light and drizzle. But in Hong Kong, the lights hid serious problems. I couldn't possibly judge how the insides of the buildings looked, or how many people lived there with their families, but from the outside, the apartments oozed sadness and repressed frustration through the worn-out window frames.

Journeys start and end with doors. Between them you have only noise. The university campus was the only quiet place I found in Hong Kong. As soon as one stepped into the railway station, you'd get sucked into the noise, sensations, impressions, of the soulless, hyperactive city. The only moment you can think about what just happened is when you come back to your room. The rest was white noise and a foreign language.

I don't know when I started spending so much time with Fei-yan before people started gossiping. We were living in the same block, and after our meeting at the art studios, we bumped into each other almost everywhere around campus: grocery shops, canteens, libraries, and even classes. I was proud that I could recognize Fei-yan's face, and as the days went on, I was beginning to wonder where I'd meet her next. Just like before, when we chased each other around the factory, only I wasn't pretending to be annoyed when I saw her smiling and waving. After those five seconds, both of us went about our business, but as soon as she passed by me, I'd get a sense of sweet memory, like meeting somebody I used to know a long time ago. Even though our conversations, mostly in the elevator, were brief, small talk, the voice, the lips, teeth, and tongue working together to form opinions and questions, they were charged with a meaning I couldn't get.

She sat next to me during one of the classes. We didn't talk at all during the lecture. After it was over, I said I wanted to eat. Fei-yan was hungry as well. She picked the place and ordered some lunch.

During our talk, I found out she was a graduate student. She studied quantitative finance and then moved to literature, she was from the mainland, she had no brothers and sisters, and she wouldn't let others sit on her bed. Not even herself if she hadn't showered and dressed in clean pajamas. She also found out that I was an undergrad, studying in Amsterdam but I'm not Dutch, I have a sister, and I don't have problems with other people on my bed. We talked and talked, she laughed and laughed, and we had a nice lunch. She was making me feel smart but I couldn't figure if she was genuinely into the conversation or just making fun of a foreigner. She also told me there were other lectures and seminars I could go to if I was interested in them.

I don't know exactly when we started eating together every day. We talked about literature, about books, about authors, gossip, and "did you know" moments, and we even introduced each other to some writers from back home. She made me feel smart. ******

Literature was one of the few subjects he was interested in, and Fei-yan noticed how Guy's face across the table lightened up. He started making hand gestures whenever either of them brought up the topic. She was happy to talk about such things with the foreigner. Even though he did most of the talking and was awkward at times, Fei-yan was a good listener. Even though he asked her a couple of times to contribute to the conversation, she simply smiled, because she liked to hear him talk. Of course, the guy felt uneasy, and of course, Fei-yan had answers to all his questions, yet she took a strange sense of pleasure once the guy became aware of the silence and then just talked some more to dispel it. His main concern, though, was how to keep it going to prevent the crushing silence from settling in. It was white noise most of the time, constantly directing one's actions towards the speaker. The guy laughed at some point and said she talked a lot through her eyes and smile. When it was necessary, Fei-yan would often say something elusive, almost poetic. The guy, then, made something out of it and then kept the conversation going. It was like blowing into a fire that wasn't blazing, but not completely dead. He said he wasn't used to this type of talking. The guy was a good listener, too. It's just that she was better at it.

Once Fei-yan started eating with the guy almost every day, they would no longer bump into each other around campus. But she thought it was a nice trade-off. She hoped that all those conversations they had over lunch, breakfast, and dinner would make him tell his story. The look in his eye, the way something sad came over him even when he was smiling intrigued her. And he also wrote! Of course, the guy, like so many other men from two different continents, liked her, otherwise he wouldn't talk to her that much. The guy wanted to know why she made the jump from finance to literature and ever since Fei-yan told him that after the art studios trip, the guy turned the questions on all sides in his head. He was just too shy to ask.

"The most valuable gift you can give someone is your time," Fei-yan said at one of their meals. The guy couldn't quite get where she was going, but Fei-yan was haunted by that line. While Guy was still thinking, Fei-yan remembered her family and awkward dinner conversations on boyfriends.

The female human body has around four hundred eggs that

are eliminated one by one every month. The eggs are stored inside from the time of birth, Fei-yan read in a book not so long ago. The biological course of the female is to protect the eggs and find someone suitable for them to be fertilized by. Her eggs showed how important time was. The clock was ticking, and there she was, talking literature with some blue-eyed, dark-haired foreigner instead of finding someone suitable. Guy was still trying to interpret Fei-yan's line, but she stopped listening.

The clock was ticking with her studies too. This was her last semester and she had to hand in her thesis. Fei-yan had no idea what she was going to write. Her supervisor, on the other hand, was calm about it and said there were still three and a half eggs to go. ******

I have strange dreams of gouging my eyes out, sharp objects and cutlery piercing my pupils and throwing myself in front of the trains. Buildings reaching out to each other, as if leaning for a kiss, people loaded into trucks and taken away, a young man who looked like me played with his vipers, his eyes were blue. People paint everything in black. I'm curious how fast everything would be over if I just took two steps over the yellow line. Very often in my dreams I turn away from the trains, just so I won't do it. But I poke my eyes out and wander around.

What was Carina up to? We didn't talk for some days. Is she going to wait for me at the airport? How much will both of us have changed? We fight, not talk these days. I am physically sick whenever I read her messages. Back in Amsterdam, we were trapped in our walls, we had common enemies and dishes to wash. But here, thousands of kilometers away, it's easier to say hurtful things.

Neither of us was feeling well. Like many times before in our skirmishes, guilt hugged my shoulders. I was guilty, but knowing her, she would have shaken the guilt away if our places were switched.

I hate getting into fights, especially with the people I care about. For Carina, the fight was over, the moment we agreed to make peace, but for me, I would twist and turn and think: What happened, what went wrong this time, how could I avoid this, how could I make it better? Carina knew (and was annoyed) by the way I analyzed things, and whenever she felt like it, she would round up some of her troops in an all-familiar power-game just to ruin the rest of my day.

And that's how our online conversations went. It was around 1:00 and I had class in the morning. Five minutes later, a text on my phone: *"Tea at my place? Take the stairs there are cameras in the elevator."*

I jumped out of bed.

Carina?

                                    Yeah?

how's it going?

                                    Good, idk u?

i'm fine
hanging around

                    Its been 21 days since you left me
                                    22 your time
                    You cant imagine how hard its been for me
                    You left such a mess in my room
                                    5 bags of garbage
                                    31 dishes
                    14 pieces of cutlery

...

                    It was 18 degrees in my room when I opened the door
                                    I didnt deserve this
                                    Why did you do this?
                                    Why?
                    I hope youre having fun in asia
                    Did you meet nice girls?

i'm sorry

                                    Sorry?
                                    Thats it?

what more do you want? i'm not there

                                    Thats all you can do?

Im sick to my stomach when I talk to you
I throw up after I talk to you
Do you understand?

fine then
guess i won't talk to you anymore

Im going to the therapist
You left me
I have nobody
And I have to solve your problems now
5 large bags of garbage
Our last breakfast was still on the table
Rotten food

rotten like me?

Yes rotten like you.

i can't do this anymore

Do you still feel were together?

what do you mean?

Yes or no

but it's not like i'm gone forever
ill be back soon
ill bring you something nice from hk

I dont need you to buy me things
All the time when I wanted to get out
You always bought me some nice things
Like a bracelet flowers
And it forced me to behave nicely to you

so this is about politeness?
you were behaving nice to ne because i got you things?
me*

You were forcing me to act nice
And I didnt want to say bad things
Because I didnt want to upset you

if i have to buy you things to be with me
next time i'm going to the red light district
then i'll get what i paid for

Sure.
:)
Everybody wins this way

fine then i guess we're done here
I hate you for what you did to me
With all my heart
Hope youre having fun and not coming back

really?
is that how you want to end it?
i'm gone for a couple of months
i'll be back soon
why can't you be happy for me?

I wanted to go there
Not you
You dont deserve anything
no, you don't deserve anything

Youre an outlier
Youre not supposed to be theerw
there*
but i am
get over it

I cant
I have your shit to deal with

what shit?

The room
U leaving me
I will be happy again
I promise

                                        Im going to Prague
                                        Make friends there
good for you i don't care

                                        I will make friends
                                    I will be happy without you
                                        Ill never forgive
                                        What youve done

i don't care

                                    And when youll be back
                                    Nobody will be your friend
                                        You will be alone
                                        Like I am now
                                        Yes or no?

yes or no what?

                                    Do you feel weretogether now?
                                    22 days passed since you left me

yes, i still think
we are together.
                                                    Were not
                                                    You left me
                                                    Im talking to you
                        It says your name there in white over blue
                                                    But its not you
                                                    You left me
                                                    Youre just a name
                                                    Typing
                                            Making me wanna puke
                                            Youre just an image now
                                    How do I know what youre doing?

i'm telling you what i'm doing
if you weren't so busy telling me
i make you puke

I need you here
Now
Physically
Understand?
I need u to hold me
And do things to me
In our bed

carina...

Naked
I need u to take care of your pussy
Have some fun
Pull my thorns
Be my sheep Little Prince eat me all
Be my worm Solitude eat me from the inside
Cut my wings
Cut my petals
I am the prostitute in your temple
Do me
Praise me

i need you to calm down, carina

And then we can watch shows
And well never leave our bed
Again
I cant worship a name on a blue strip
I need to be freed

carina, please stop

Im not stopping
Cum on
Tell me how much you want me
How hard are u thinking about me
How much u miss me
How you cant breathe without me
Being so far from me drives u crazy
Right?

:)
carina, I don't miss you
not sure what should reply to that
i'm in hong kong now
i'll be back soon
you're just clingy
needy
it's time for you to stand on your own two legs

                                          So you dont miss me?
                                            U dont want me?

no

                                                 Fine then :)
                                        Hope youre having fun
                                    FUCKING CHINESE GIRLS
                                          I HATE YOU SO MUCH
                                                 YOU LEFT ME
                                                     LEFT ME
                       IM SO SICK BECAUSE OF YOU RIGHT NOW
                                            I feel like dying
                       I wish u a wondeful semester abroad
                                                  wonderful*
                                                  Wonderful

take care of yourself
please

                                                       I will
                                          Dont worry about me
                                      Be sure to use a condom
                                                  Good night
                                      22 days since you left
                                                   173 to go
                                                 4152 hours
                                                    Fuck you

bye.

"**W**hy are you here?" Fei-yan said.
"What do you mean why am I here? You texted me."

"No, no, why are you *here*? People who travel this far are either too adventurous, or running away from something. What are you running from?"

"How do you know I'm not an adventurer?"

"Self-illusion can be harmful, Ulysses."

Her questions pushed me to a place I didn't want to go. But the tea was already brewing, and the cups, small and green like the petals of a flower carbonized after a volcanic eruption, were sitting on a table between us. I decided to stay. She invited me to take a seat at a safe distance from the bed.

"So nobody can sit here?"

"No."

"What if you have more than one person in your room?"

"Then they can sit on the floor. It is clean."

I couldn't believe it. When I asked her what would happen if I just got up and jumped on her bed, she smiled and said I didn't want to see her angry. Now I wanted to stay even more.

"So why am I here?"

Fei-yan realized she might have been rash with these questions the moment the guy entered. She sought to improve. Guy should feel privileged that she invited him in at such a late hour. Others – perhaps even he – might get the wrong idea.

"I cannot sleep," she said.

"And how is green tea going to help?"

"I think I had too much, that is why. I need to write my thesis by the end of this semester and I thought I would talk about it with you. Are you going to talk to me? I have tea and biscuits, and you sleep so late. Ever since I came back from Europe I cannot adjust my sleeping pattern."

"What about the rules, then? No visitors past midnight. We could get into trouble."

"Are you going to talk to me or not?"

Defeated by her straightforwardness, I said I would do what I could to help her. She went to the pantry to get the tea – the pot was the same colour as the cups. She laid some small supports that looked like toothpick rafts on the table and placed the cups on them. There was something about the way in which she poured the tea, something like a long-lost grace only Asian women had. I thanked her and looked at the cup.

Fei-yan told me about a Chinese writer named Eileen Chang, and her plans on writing her thesis about her work. I had no idea who Eileen Chang was or what was she writing about. All I could do was to give her general pieces of advice and perhaps some other things to read. Her request made me feel unusually good about myself, and the memory of the previous conversation with Carina went away. I also enjoyed her green tea. I guess the aftertaste was lodged alongside those childhood memories where you can only remember colours and images. I took another sip, bit the biscuit in silence. I forgot what we were talking about, and it was Fei-yan's turn to feel uneasy in the silence.

The tea and the biscuit played their part. The sips were gradually losing their magic, and yet the charred petal-cups that held the liquid stirred something in my mind, a something that I could no longer hold back. Deep down, in a zone of the brain called *striatum*, memories were becoming more and more restless. And I begin again to ask myself what it could have been, what triggered this response, the state where consciousness and time painfully melted into nostalgic memories. Was I drugged or dreaming? No, of course not, I was in the same room with Fei-yan at an inappropriate time, we were having tea and talking literature. And there she was, sitting next to me on her table, delighted and simultaneously confused that I enjoyed her tea in silence.

The thing that started twitching was Hollowness itself reaching back to me. The tastes, the splashes of colour, the sound- bites and gentle touches were throwing me into a state of confusion and shame. Trying to break off the silence, Fei-yan said there is an old Chinese proverb where, "There is a price for gold but none for good tea." I could have said that the same goes for women: There is a price for sex but not for love, but I didn't want to make it awkward. Looking outside her window to the neighbourhood beyond the water, I nodded. The tea was starting to wear off.

"What were you thinking?"

"It's just that I remembered a scene with a French guy

having some tea and cookies and then going on for seven books or so."

"I bet you get many girls with your references, right?"

Silence.******

"Maybe every man has had two such women – at least two. Marry a red rose and eventually she'll be a mosquito-blood streak smeared on the wall, while the white one is 'moonlight in front of my bed.' Marry a white rose, and before long she'll be a grain of sticky rice that's got stuck to your clothes; the red one, by then, is a scarlet beauty mark just over your heart."

Fei-yan made me listen to one of her favourite quotes from Eileen Chang's book. Firstly, she liked it because she couldn't figure out what kind of rose she was going to change into when married, and second, the choice of one rose over another was time-dependent. No matter which rose you would pick, you'd have to make peace with the fact that things change. It was almost like a strategy game where you had to think a couple of moves in advance. But ultimately, it was unlikely for Fei-yan to experience both roses. Just like her four hundred eggs, she thought, you are either one rose or the other the moment you are born. When she showed the quote to the guy next to her, he was intrigued by the images Eileen Chang picked for her love metaphor, and how everything was so pragmatic. Fei-yan was slightly disappointed the guy couldn't pick up the time thing. "Time goes by so slow in Europe!" and just got stuck with the exotic. The conversation was going right where she wanted.

"So which type of rose are you, Fei-yan?"

"Depends on who's asking."

"Fine then."

Your clouded face, Fei-yan.

"You are a very annoying character, you know that? Why are you giving up so easily? Why are you so *passive*? It seems life is *always* elsewhere for you. Why so? What is wrong with you?"

"I could ask you the same thing. You did finance, then went on to study literature – how did that happen? Why did you do it?"

"Do you want to share stories? Fine then," she said pouring me another cup of tea. "Stay with me and hear what I have to say."

"It is funny how people change once they are in a foreign country," Fei-yan said. "I came back from a trip to Europe this winter. I liked the food, I liked Paris, I liked walking around the same streets or going to the cafés or bookstores like writers used to. I could not explain why, but as soon as I stepped out of the airplane, bus, train, or whatever, I was attracted, like a magnet. It was impossible to explain, but the old buildings were charged with the spirits of all the people that had lived there before, and as time went on, almost nothing changed – only the clothing styles and the cars. The same shops, the same people, the same problems, and the same small talk in funny languages everywhere you go. I liked that in Europe: a warmth that you do not get anywhere else. It is funny how the West perceives the East as a slow-moving place with all those nice images of pagodas and old Chinese masters who teach martial arts and eat rice dumplings and have funny accents when talking English. With all your old buildings, I thought Europe was the place where time stood still and everyone just hangs out at a pub or café every chance they get. Of course, I was only a tourist and like all tourists, I just wanted to fulfill the expectations I made reading all those travel guides and watching all those French movies."

"Look outside," she said pointing towards the neighbourhood outside her window. "There is no soul in Hong Kong. Only giant concrete penises and very rich and very poor people living in closed communities. I hate Hong Kong, I hate its obsession with success. That is why Asian people will never take over the world, like all paranoid Westerners seem to believe. When I was around ten or eleven, my parents forced me to play the piano. I know, I know, a stereotype. And I was pretty good at it and went to competitions. But I guess as soon as you get serious about something, it just loses its charm. So there I was at this contest, and a French child who had a technique worse than mine and practiced half the time I did somehow managed to move the audience in a way I could never have hoped to do. In the end, he won the competition. Crying my eyes out, I asked my instructor what I did wrong, I played perfectly and yet the French child took the prize. My teacher tried to answer me (but what can you answer a ten-year-old when she asks you such a thing?) and in the end he said that sometimes playing perfectly is not enough. I wanted to quit playing, but my parents insisted and pressured me to continue. Like the good daughter I was, I listened to them and lost the second, the third, and even the fourth time. There was no chance for me as a pianist, so I quit."

"But that is where I want to get to," Fei-yan continued. "Do not get me wrong, I love my country, I love my culture, you should see how fired up I get whenever it comes to China and its politics and I am sure there are things I can show you. But despite that, there is something about you, about Europe that I really like. *Something*, a spark of creativity, and a better way of expressing yourselves, I do not know. That is what I have learned from my trip to Europe, trying to figure out why I kept losing. There is a lost beauty and romanticism that somehow becomes attractive in what it means to be European and perhaps that is where you draw your strength from."

"I have considered myself a foreigner all my life. I lived in China in middle school, moved to Singapore, and now I am stuck here. Once you move around, especially when you are younger, you tend to wrap yourself in a shell. Being tough is not necessarily a bad thing; it allows you to judge in a serious way, like a grown-up. Although I was proved wrong and not just once, I was stubborn and believed that being cold about life was the way to do it. Things were simple: from A to B to C to D. I looked down on other people who were not following the code: it was their fault for not trying hard enough, not some external cause. To me, complaining or finding excuses were just weak attempts to evade the hard work, the A to B to C to D."

Fei-yan took a sip of tea and sat back in her chair. As I motioned her with my eyes to go on, she poured me another cup and handed another biscuit. I liked how she pronounced the words, rounded and clear like the news.

"It all became clear when I traveled to Europe. Of all the cities I have been to, Prague was the nicest. As you can see on my wall, most pictures I took were from Prague and Charles Bridge. That is where all became clear."

Fei-yan stopped for a moment, giving me time to look at the pictures on her wall. When she started talking again, I turned my head to her. I did not tell her I was from Prague.

"I knew something was out of place as soon as I did not see

that band playing on the bridge," she said pointing towards another picture. "Then, I decided to go and see Kafka's monument, do you know it? The empty suit with Kafka on top? (I nodded.) I was walking towards it, with my map in my hand, but it was not there. I swear, I was standing *right* in the place where it should be, but it was gone. That was one of the moments when I lost reality and the things around me. Maybe there was something wrong with the map, maybe I was not in the right place, but as soon as I started looking around, all the people were naked and on top of their clothes. Like invisible men dressed in cotton or linen, both tourists and locals were riding their clothes like it was the most normal thing in the world. I looked at myself and started panicking, but I still had my clothes on. It was a weird show. The people on top of their clothes looked like they had veils drawn over their eyes, like blind people. They were walking around Prague, mindlessly taking pictures of every single building. They were filming other people walking around, they were taking group pictures, even of their coffees or dishes. Always with a blank look.

"Sometimes, there is nothing more grotesque than a human body. Of course, there are all these billboards with pretty models, and people told me I look a bit like Zhang Ziyi, the famous Chinese actress, but seeing all those naked people walking about in Prague disgusted me. Chest hairs, sweaty armpits, cellulite, c-sectioned tummies, fat, splayed feet, acne eruptions on their backs, amputated limbs, receding hairlines, horrible tumours, atrophied leg muscles from sitting in wheelchairs, and many other horrible images. I can see them right now. At least Kafka had the decency to put clothes on while climbing his suit. After I ran back to my hotel room, crying, I knew why I lost the piano competitions. The French child played worse than me. That was a fact. But it's precisely that *lack* of precision that moved the imprecise ears of the audience. We like imperfection, and the more we try to hide it, the uglier we seem. But seeing all that imperfection scared me. It is just like in your story with Adam and Eve after they ate the apple. They began hiding the things they were ashamed of. But not in Prague. Their shame was right there for me to see.

"My technique was flawless, but at the same time there was something lacking. And that is why you Europeans are, in a way, superior. You do not try to hide your small defects, you do not try to run away, you embrace them, you accept the *difference* and use it to your advantage. The Chinese, the way I see it, are better at hiding their shame. Of course, this is too simple, and as an educated person I should not say that, but it is the only way I can make you understand. In that moment of terror when Prague showed me something that reminded me of Kafka, that was when I had everything for a second and then lost it back in Hong Kong. We are *different*. In Hong Kong, everyone wants to get rich and fly to Europe on holidays.

"When I came back from Europe, I never adjusted my sleeping pattern to Hong Kong. Ever since I got here, I only go to bed early in the morning. The trip changed me, but sadly, it makes Hong Kong and the people around me seem more strange than before. I hope you will not feel the same in future, when you go back to Amsterdam. I lost something for *understanding* and I am not sure I could get it back even if I were to return to Prague.

"That is why you are here. That is why you are in my room, drinking tea with me at an inappropriate hour. That is why I answered my question for you. Coming back, I sadly realized that A to B to C to D is not the guaranteed way to success. There is also imperfection, difference. And I took it upon myself to try to talk more to other people. You see, that is what makes you interesting. You are the first European I have met who hides something. Usually, when I meet Europeans, you know their story in the first ten minutes, but you are not like that. You are a strange European as much as I am a strange Asian, and here we are, in a city that is not the same as China, but which is also not a city in the West. It is funny to watch you talk. You see me smiling all the time, you hear me talking, even when it is absolutely necessary. It is only natural you create this image of this silly, shallow, giggling Chinese girl. I never told this story about Prague to anyone. I like hearing you talk, but you are not telling me everything.

"So, when are you going to climb on top of your clothes?"

C arina couldn't get rid of my smell no matter how much she cleaned the room. Dishes, laundry, changing the bed sheets, sweeping, scrubbing the floor and there was still something that reminded her of me: thirty-one dishes, five large garbage bags, 6.3 kilos of laundry, and the bed sheet with three large stripes. She was going back to Prague in eighteen days. Carina was feeling better from all the cleaning even though she didn't manage to scrub me away. She needed to focus, to gather herself from all that mess. But I shouldn't be talking about this right now because Carina is going to have another of those "attacks." From time to time, she would stop and get scared for no reason. Last time she did it was when she talked to me over Facebook. Her heart started feeling strange, her whole body trembled, her ears heard a rumbling noise like an industrial hammer (or a song by Tim Hecker), and her face, ugly with fear and pain, looked as if she saw a ghost. And maybe it was a real ghost there, crawling along the corner of her room in ragged clothes. But then the fear would pass, and she would go about her day.

Carina couldn't get rid of my smell in the room because Solitude was wearing one of my old shirts. Carina never liked my body odour, did you, Carina? She said it was too powerful and always tried to get rid of it – special shower gels, strong detergents, persistent perfumes. Whenever I came back home from the gym or wore a shirt for a couple of days in a row, Carina couldn't bear smelling – not to mention touching – my pieces of clothing. Sweatiness repulsed Carina as much as morning breath. She was a bit sensitive – that was all.

Solitude got hold of one of my shirts, and whenever it would crawl past Carina it would leave a trail. Carina would throw the dish away and follow the smell up to the moment where it got lost. She was sent in this quest around her room countless times – maybe there was something like a dirty sock or an old rag I used to wipe my face with, thrown away under the bed or in the sock drawer or on the bookshelves maybe. She could find nothing and her "attacks" started up over again. The worm inside her brain laughed at her, every chance it got: *"Stupid! You're chasing him in your room while he's chasing chicks in Hong Kong. Worthless. That's what you are."*

Whenever Carina had an attack, Solitude would snort and

clap. How easy it was to start her off! Whenever she left the room, Solitude took its usual spot in the corner, waiting. They all come back, Carina, they all do. While gone, Solitude would make my smell more persistent and Carina's memories more powerful. No matter how much Carina tried to get on with her life, now that I wasn't there, no matter the twenty-seven minutes she would stop thinking about Hong Kong per day, the moment she stepped into her room, she pictured the first moment she was greeted by Solitude. Sometimes the memory was so strong that some nights she didn't even dare go inside, locking the door and running as fast as she could in the empty hallways. After some time (Carina calculated the longest time she spent being afraid of entering her room was forty-seven minutes plus the elevator ride), she worked up the courage to go back and try to get some sleep. Solitude, welcoming Carina back like an old friend, crept up next to her. They always slept together and Carina often found herself snuggling it as if it was somebody else. Solitude wrapped around Carina and from this angle it looked like she was being swallowed whole, like a white blood cell eating bacterium. Late at night, when Carina woke up in fear with her eyes half-closed (she could still see the clock showing 2:02 AM), Solitude took on my face and my voice saying, "It's okay, just go back to sleep."

Once a week, Carina went to group therapy with Solitude. Every morning, Carina had to think what to do, where to go, what is the temperature today, but Solitude would hold her tighter, his eyes were blue, and say do nothing and go nowhere, easy enough. The sheets and the blanket clutched her tighter. When Carina finally got out of the shower, something still smelled like me, like Solitude, like a few missed opportunities, and opening doors to cold rooms, Carina. She ate less, skipped breakfast and coffee, and heard the same things from her therapist over and over again. Yes, she was being more positive, yes she did things that made her feel better, yes she was enjoying the time spent with Solitude, no, they didn't try colouring books for adults, no, they still sleep in the same bed and do everything together. Carina would put her hands to her ears and it was like sinking into a bathtub.

You wanted to be free, Carina, you told that to your therapist and you drew patterns all over the edge of the chair, but every time you said that, the therapist said the session was over, and he knew, Solitude knew, Carina, that you sank your fingers in that leather, that nice leather that covered the chair and the 50 euros per session and then you said "Fine!" and slammed the door. You weren't hungry, you wanted to do things on your own, even if the worm always told you that without Solitude you'll be nothing, and everybody waited for you to cave in, everyone wanted you back in bed with Solitude to swallow you up.

The bed was the only place where she could feel safe in the whole room. Unlike me, Solitude didn't snore.

I woke up from Fei-yan's story minutes after she stood there in complete silence just like I would wake up from a dream. I looked around her room, her closed drawer, her nicely-kept bed, the desk where she worked, the pictures of her family, her books. The tea became more diluted every time she poured hot water in the teapot. We both stayed quiet. She smiled and stroked her hair a couple of times, trying to invite me to contribute to our intimacy. The room was filled with silence for what seemed like years.

"I will ask again. Why are you here?"

"I don't know, I am studying abroad."

"But why? Why Hong Kong?"

"I just came here on a whim. I didn't plan it."

"Does your family miss you?"

"I guess."

"Did you leave someone behind?"

"Haven't we all?"

She frowned.

"Just a couple friends, nothing much."

"Does this conversation bother you?"

"Not really."

"Were you always like this?"

"What do you mean?"

"Did you always talk like this?"

"I don't remember."

"How were you as a child?"

"Like all childhoods, mine was just a mixture of feelings, colours, sensations, discoveries, and playing football in the courtyard behind the apartment block where my family lived."

She asked me to keep going.

"As I'm sure there were countless people telling you how pretty or beautiful you are, so have other people told me I was special. Now, before you start giggling, I wasn't special in that awful kind of way. No, they were expecting me to do great things at some point in my life. And everybody was so sure about this that it put me off. Even as a kid I knew I had something other kids around me didn't have, and secretly I was proud of it. But at the same time, I *wanted* to be a part of their group, I wanted to play with them, to laugh, to do the things all the kids do. Because of this "gift," I had to try to be normal. But like all good actors, it's hard to separate yourself from your characters after a while. I had a third eye inside my skull. That made me special. And with this third eye, I could see right into people, I could pick up small gestures, small hints that would give them away. I could read people like they were a text scrolling down on the surface of their bodies. I was fascinated by it. I couldn't tell anyone, I tried a couple of times, but then a kid I thought I was close to started laughing in such an evil way that it ripped my heart up. I was being so honest with him, maybe that's why he started laughing so loud, made fun of me and then went on to kick the ball in the concrete courtyard. I never heard a person laughing with such pure evil. I don't know, kids can be like that sometimes. After I told him about my superpower, he didn't talk to me again, and I could see him peeking at me from across the courtyard with a mixture of fear and disgust.

"Figuring out I was some sort of genius or artist (I never said I had an illness or something), I tried reading and writing. It started with a couple of books. Then a few more, and then I could picture the whole thing that was presented to me inside my skull. With paintings and movies, everything is out there for you, but in this case, it becomes something else. Then I tried writing myself. Like a weaving spider, I would sit at my table and write, ignoring everything and everyone around. It didn't matter what or who I was writing about. I felt powerful, I felt I could make people live or die. That kid I just mentioned a minute ago? For example, I could tell you, 'He was laughing at me and he was so evil his face melted and turned into a demon with worms spewing out of his mouth,' I could just as well have said 'He disappeared, he never came back and he said he likes boys,' or I don't know. I could mould anything and anyone into what I wanted."

Fei-yan could only smile and nod in approval. She was startled.

I continued.

"Of course, writing wasn't easy. I was trying to use my inner eye, to translate the things I was seeing and I secretly hoped I could write and tell some of the greatest stories ever. Artists can be young and proud like that. Writing in that small notebook, I could feel it breathing, I could feel its pulse and the small organs taking shape. I wanted to write *everything*. Sure, there are lots of words behind *everything*, and there were many places and people in my story, but all I wanted was to replace myself. I was creating the universe in my notebook, I gave it the breath of life only so that at the right time, I would get sucked into it, merge with it, wrap myself in the tissues of that notebook, and completely disappear from this world and live in my own. My pages were Truth and I, their servant. A tool through which a pagan god was talking. I believed in those pages with the fervour of a religious extremist, that's how I was so sure I was going to be promised an afterlife.

"I was wrong. I was arrogant, like a statue. I showed a part of my *everything* to one of my literature teachers, and he wasn't as pleased as I was. He said I was doing too much explaining, too much managing, it's unclear, the characters aren't well-defined, confusing, I was *trying too hard*. But I shouldn't despair, my teacher assured me. I'm still young, and if I want to pursue this whole writing business, I must write as much as possible, and continue writing every single day. While he said that he patted my head the way a parent would do. I'm sure he meant well, but I hated him so much I didn't show him anything at all after that. In fact, I stopped showing my writing to anyone, and when I'm dead in some basement, the people will find me holding on to my notebook. But then, why write if you have nobody to show it to? Everyone, and I mean *everyone* who writes, paints, writes music or something like that *wants* people to read, listen, or gaze in amazement, otherwise there's no purpose in doing so. I was writing because I was feeling hollow and once people read me, they would accept me and look at me as if I were this sacred monster.

"The eye inside my skull is unreliable," I kept on with what I had to say. "The stories were terrible, just like I said over coffee a few days ago. That doesn't mean I hate my teacher any less. If I had any superpower when I was younger, now it's just gone. My eye doesn't understand what it sees. But I'm happy, because otherwise I would meet the expectations of the people who placed their faith in me that I would go great things. Since my eye was shut, I've been haunted by Hollowness. The eye can't be fully closed, nor can it be completely open. It's like you feel returned from heaven. You know you had something at one point, something beautiful, but doubt creeps in and transforms itself into Hollowness. That's why you noticed me, that's why, I think, you wanted to hear my story so badly. I have one foot in the divine and another in the mud. This passiveness is my Hollowness. How would you be, if you had something and one day it's gone? That's why you think I'm a strange European. I can't be naked in front of other people, and even if I would tell you my "standard European" story, like where I'm from, what kind of beer or wine I like or show you pictures of my family, that still wouldn't be enough for you, right?"

She nodded.

"I can't embrace my defects; I mean, I still hate my teacher even though I know he was right. That tells you something, I hope. And so, I'm in a constant search for myself, I'm trying to feed the Hollowness. It's not an easy thing, looking for yourself. What is there to find if the pedestal that lifts your core is empty?

"In the end, I don't know exactly why I'm here. I didn't want to come in the first place, and I'll tell you the story another time, it's a good one, but I hope to find the same things you did when you came to Prague, to Europe. Maybe that's how things are meant to be, some things are *supposed* to happen. I'm trying to find myself. Maybe I can find something to please Hollowness here, in the city that's filled with pricks. But how should I know, since my coming here was the result of a higher power and a strange dream, like someone else, some pagan, blue-eyed, dark-haired god is sitting at his desk wearing striped pajamas, caffeined out of his mind and typing away, twisting our fates in ways we didn't believe possible, laughing at it. Maybe somewhere along the way this god broke into my room and looked at my notebooks and decided there was something valuable after all. Who knows what I am meant to find here who knows about my blind wandering except you and the someone who's writing me into being? And who knows what will come of us without any divine intervention?

"Fiction or no fiction, traveling is a good plot device. Your tea hardly tastes like tea anymore."

"ell me another story," Fei-yan asked me with her eyes as she made another pot of tea.

"It's a bit late, don't you think?"

"I've got time. Are you tired?"

"Not really, it's just I'm giving away too much for one night," I tried to defend myself.

"Why are you so closed? I am sure you must have other stories that show how vulnerable and sad you are. Is it not much easier to tell your stories to strangers?"

"I don't know, are you a stranger?" I pretended not to understand her.

Another minute of complete silence. I was relieved and stupid after I finished, and I was watching Fei-yan pour tea in our cups with the timeless grace that only Europeans think Asian women have. We barely knew each other, why was I so awkward about it? But Fei-yan seemed pleased by it.

I took another sip and felt the rattling inside my brain, but not as strong as the first time. Fei-yan took out some raisins and almonds, and placed the plate on the table beside the teapot. In a water glass there were two small bamboo trees the size of asparagus stalks. One of them had a withered tip.

"I do not know why, but my plants are dying. Bamboos are so easy to maintain, they grow everywhere. I guess I am not that good at keeping plants. I view this dying bamboo the way I would view myself. After you reach a certain age, I guess, everything slowly withers. You are constantly trying to find something that is lost, you keep telling yourself things are alright, but at the back of your mind, you know you are lying to yourself.

"My biggest fear and at the same time my biggest frustration is how people judge me based on my pretty face. You would be surprised how many people I have turned down, how many people proposed to me, and how many more like me in secret. I can see it in your eyes you want me to give you a number, but I would not want to destroy your hopes, trust me. It is only natural, of course, if you think about it: There are so many people in China, and if you are a pretty girl, you get to go on a lot of dates. Also, there are many more guys in China than girls, so again, the numbers are on my side. Being a girl and going against my family's wishes to study literature, the only way I could make them happy again would be to marry a rich guy.

"The withering shows that I do not have time. My pretty face is not going to be pretty for long. Marriage and having children of your own is a big thing in China. It is only in recent years that we have been introduced to this 'hook-up culture,' but in the end everyone needs to marry and settle and make babies. At my age, I am already 'old.' Just like the bamboo you see here, I have started withering.

"It does not matter how many guys like me, the only ones that do matter are the ones I like back. I only had three relationships so far, and all three of them were disasters. I also never did it with any of them, and looking back, it was for the better. I like the idea of being pure before my marriage. Who does such a thing these days? Of course, it is going to be hard to share the bed. I believe there is a certain order to things, and doing it with somebody I am not going to get married to ruins this order. Chasing away these impure thoughts relieves me of this anxiety of having sex but marriage re-orders them in a nicer way, they conform and close an ideal. You see, the unity of marriage is also a unity of experience, which brings, with all its symbols and rituals, something religious. And tell me now, what European thinks this way today? You embrace your defects, that is certain, but more and more you choose to live alone or divorce and get re-married five times. It shows one of your major problems: fear of commitment, and always trying to have 'the new.' I hated those writers who married several times and the girls got younger and prettier as they were growing old or even teachers marrying their students. There is something wrong and foul, almost like incest. But I guess that is how artists work. Even in old age, they are not fully grown up and emotionally stuck around the age of eighteen. Of course, I am not trying to say that *all* Chinese do not have sex before marriage, or that all of Europe is shameless, decadent, and pollutes the purity of China. It is just the way I chose to live my life. I chose not to let anyone touch my bed unless they are worthy of it. And do not think of it in a sexual sense. Think of it as a moment even more intimate than the one we are sharing right now.

"My first boyfriend liked boys and he had a relationship with me only because he did not want to lose face in front of his friends. He was so handsome and took such good care of himself, it was only a matter of time before people started getting suspicious. You know, at that young age, I had no idea what was going on. Still, I moved on. For my next one, I chose not to go for the prettiest guy around, but the total opposite. He was ugly, fat, and played video games all day. None of my friends liked him, and every time we went out things got tense and awkward. Believe it or not, he cheated on me with this other girl who came from the States a few months into our relationship. But happily, his joy was short-lived. This girl had to go back to the States because she found a job, and when this other guy managed to scrape up the money and the visa for the US, she was having her wedding in two weeks or so. There is always a bigger fish in cheating, I always say.

Fei-yan stood up and said she needed to go to the bathroom. I nodded and had another sip of tea. I started picturing a gigantic pool filled with Fei-yan's suitors, each of them covered in mud and struggling to get out. The mess, the complete chaos settled in there was watched by Fei-yan herself, who declared that the first person to get out would receive her as a prize. I was there myself, in the middle of it. People, of all colours, races, and ages were fighting each other, stepping on each other, biting and pulling each other's hair. Some of them were annoyed at how their expensive suits were getting torn. Everyone was looking for a way out one way or another, but nobody could get out. Fei-yan was sitting outside it, encouraging and luring one or two lucky contestants who would ultimately slip back to their doom. The suitors on the bottom of the pool died a long time ago, and their bodies were arranged in layers, much like when one would cut through an old rock...

But then, something else crossed my mind. I stood up, then went to the bed. I tilted her pillow a little, and crumpled her blanket and sheet. I returned to my chair, sipping the tea.

I looked for a moment at her wall with photos, then turned and looked at the pictures of her and her family on her desk. Next to them, there was a Bavarian gingerbread heart that had written in icing "*I mog di.*" Knowing a bit of German, I figured it must be a form of "*Ich mag dich.*" I like you. Fei-yan came back and didn't notice anything. She took her seat right across me, apologizing for taking the time.

"What's with the gingerbread heart up there on your desk?" I ask.

"Oh... I bought that from my trip to Germany. It was Munich, I think."

"So you bought a gingerbread heart that says 'I like you?' You must like yourself very much. You usually receive those as a gift and they are, like they say, 'a gift from the heart.' You know you have to tell me the story of the gingerbread heart."

I crossed my arms and smiled, looking over a battle I was winning. She hesitated for a moment, looked around, trying to find her words, wanted to start a couple of times, but the words were stuck on her lips. I could tell she was a bit angry, but in the end, her eyes admitted submission and she continued.

"A year ago, I was on a trip to Cambodia. You know, we went to those famous places like Angkor Wat and Angkor Tom, and we also stayed for a couple of days in Phnom Penh. There were four of us, two girls and two guys, and the girl who was with me liked one of them, and, you know, they wanted to get together during the trip, even though she insisted there was nothing going on. But something went wrong, and the other guy, not the one my friend liked, and I had to leave the next day. During our flight, this guy confessed to me he had loved me for the past three years, and out of all the possible moments, he chose this one to tell me. You can imagine the awkwardness that followed. I smiled and thanked him for letting me know (as I usually do) that he liked me, and gave an ambiguous answer. I only wanted to get away from him as soon as possible but there were no other seats left.

"We arrived, but the other two people did not. They texted us later telling that they had already seen what was there to see, and left for Phnom Penh. The other guy and I came in pretty late, and all the buses were gone for the day, so we had to stay there overnight. I trembled at the thought of sharing a room with him and cursed my travel partners – see? People do change when you travel. I visited the ruins, but I cringed each time my colleague talked about where we were going to stay that night. In the end, we found something cheap. We settled a meeting point for the next day with the whole group, threatening them with losing our friendship if they were not there. When we finally came to our room, I left my bags and said to my travel companion that I was going for some fresh air. Obviously, he wanted to come as well since 'no girl should walk these streets at night alone.' But I said I will be back soon, and he should get ready for bed. Hoping he would take the bait, I literally ran out.

"I walked around and decided my best bet was to go to a bar, club, whatever, and stay there. And that was where I met him. He was sitting alone at a bar with a beer in front of him. As soon as I came close to the bar, he asked me if he could buy me a drink. 'Sure,' I said, and sat next to him."

Fei-yan continued.

"We talked and time seemed to go by at a nice pace for us. I was not feeling tired because of the traveling, not even angry at my friend for leaving me here, or disgusted by my travel companion who said he liked me during the plane trip. He was a bit older than I was, he lived in Munich, he was the son of a wealthy company owner, and now he was on vacation in South-East Asia. He seemed well-read (a decisive quality when it comes to men), and the way he talked fascinated me. At first, it did not look like he was interested, and I can tell when somebody is interested or not, but his gestures, his manner of speaking, the way he looked at me all told a different story. After a couple more drinks, I told him my situation and how I did not want to go back to my room until morning, and he said he was leaving for Phnom Penh in an hour or so, and if I wanted to come, there was enough room for one more.

"I knew at this point things seemed inappropriate and that everything could have gone wrong in so many ways, but the way he behaved from the moment I met him was so... charming, just like the snake in your story of Adam and Eve. I did not think about the bad things that could have happened. He was very *warm* – an unusual quality in Germans, whom you would expect to be sober, stoic, and reserved. And so, I ran back to our hostel, opened the door, took my bags – the guy was sound asleep and barely moved as I was packing up – and then went back to the car waiting outside.

"In the end, the guy convinced me I should not meet my friends at all – how could they have left me by myself with that creep just to make an excuse to get together. 'You shouldn't rely on such friends,' he warned me. In the heat of the moment, I agreed with him, and overall, I am not a forgiving person. So I texted my friends and told them we would meet in Hong Kong in a couple of days. Then I switched my phone off.

"I liked that German very much, and once the trip was over, he visited me a couple of times and he always sent small gifts in between, like this gingerbread heart. And when I went to Germany, I spent Christmas with his family – I had no idea Christmas is such a big thing in Europe where you have a 'family dinner.' His parents could not speak English and they believed I was his girlfriend and his relatives were very nice to me. All of the sudden I found myself realizing that I truly like him, you know, I could picture myself in that place, that cozy setting. It was good inside his family. And let us not forget it was Europe! The things on my checklist were being ticked off one by one, and that made me very happy.

"But life is not for happiness. In your fairy tales you have that last line *'And they lived happily ever after.'* That is one of the biggest lies. Because the guy was the son of a wealthy company owner, it was not hard for him to find me an internship in Munich in a bank. It was not exactly what I was hoping for, since I was studying finance and secretly hoped to move to literature, but nevertheless I was very excited at this thought. All of the sudden, the son of the company owner was constantly troubled by something. I made the arrangements, the visa preparations, and I told him I was coming somewhere in May. He ran his hand through his hair – I remember we were Skyping at that time – and he reached a point where he could not keep it in any longer. I asked him what was wrong, and obviously he said 'nothing.' But I was very insistent, I can be very insistent at times, and demanded answers. In the end he confessed he was seeing someone else this whole time.

"I was not sure what to feel," Fei-yan said after a short pause, as if trying to remember. "If he said his ex-girlfriend was paying him a visit or something like that, then it is not so much of a problem, right? The relationship did not work out and you move on. Maybe in some cases you actually 'stay friends.' I, for one, do not believe that, but hiding it, acting like everything is normal when it comes to such matters is something that can hardly be looked over. It is not only the lying or 'omission' as he used to call it. But when you 'omit' this it shows a huge personality flaw. He was, like you said, hollow. There was something inside his being that was wrong from the beginning. Of course, I was not planning on marrying (at least, not in the short-term), and I guess if he would have explained some things from the beginning I would have understood. But when you have another other, you might find it hard to balance both situations. His plan, I think, was to let it all slip by until the next clear water. But how far can you get? Maybe they were planning on getting married and having children. There is something terribly disturbing with having two mothers for your children. This is something only a paranoid woman would think, but in reality I was looking for a reason to hate him even more. The idea of having a child with a man who might have had one repulsed me like the most disgusting thing on the planet. For me, love *is* time. We are not going to be around here forever. I did not tell you these stories just to brag of my (failed) relationships, I just wanted to show you how important time is and how I had some bad time investments. Time is not something that can be measured by your clocks. Time *is* everything. And because it is so limited, it is the most precious gift you can give to somebody.

"I stopped talking to him – he still sends small gifts from time to time, he calls me, texts me, writes to me, but I never respond. From that point onwards, anything he did or said was false. I keep that gingerbread heart on my desk as a memory that even 'a gift from the heart,' like you said, can be rotten inside – just like the dough or the icing and the concrete heart of Hong Kong."

L ing Fei-yan finished her story and her tea. The room sank in silence, as if the walls were sponges trying to absorb every single word that was said during the time she talked without stopping. We were crossing some borders we weren't supposed to and tried to fill spaces too large for this room.

"I'm sorry," I said, "I shouldn't have asked about the gingerbread heart."

"It is fine. I guess you cannot stop a story once you start telling it."

"What time is it?"

"Early in the morning. Care for some more tea?"

"I think that's enough for tonight."

I left Fei-yan's room and snuck back to mine. Images of people I barely knew were walking me down the stairs. Fei-yan wanted to talk forever. It was hard to fall asleep and I found myself watching the sunrise over the mountains and the neighbourhood beyond the water. We were gulping time like hot tea. Still trying to fall asleep and still trying to figure out what to make of the things I just heard, I was happy. Fei-yan and I shared something and both of us wanted to know more. Layer by layer, we would peel each other until nothing was left. For the first time, I had someone I could *talk* to in this unreal city.

The sun started clearing the brown fog of a winter dawn. A crowd flowed over the bridge into the trains that carried them to work. I had not thought trains carried so many.

Hollowness was already in my bed, greeting me like an old friend. It lifted the blanket just so I could get back in. It's been a while since we last slept together. I squeezed it in my arms like I would squeeze Carina.

I had strange dreams that morning. I didn't go to class and felt nauseous all day.

Carina didn't like Prague and all the work preparations for the student conference kept her from doing all the things the other tourists do when in Prague: The Charles Bridge, Old Town, the rivers, the parties, and classical music. The thing she hated the most was the opulence in the architecture – it somehow tried too hard to put all of Europe in a single city, and anyone who thought they could experience the whole of Europe from visiting Prague is a "0". She barely remembered meeting her family for dinner in town. She couldn't stand seeing them, seeing her parents judging her for not going abroad. Her parents asked if she's alright, and Carina answered she's very busy – she worked until late at night, and during the day she acted as the guide for the rest of the group, that's why she stayed at the hotel, and not at her parents' place. They didn't bother asking for more than this.

Carina prepared five reports of two thousand words each. She'd often do the work of her group, and everyone was okay with that. The other people who accompanied her from Amsterdam did their touristy job while Carina had a perfect excuse not to go around the city. Even though she wasn't in Amsterdam anymore, Solitude was always there for Carina. The worm mocked her, saying *"Your ex-boyfriend is in Hong Kong and you're doing other people's work like some Filipino slave. You should throw away all that crap you're studying and start working in a sweatshop!"* But Carina's therapist encouraged her not to listen to what the worm was saying and just do the things she was most content with. The therapist also prescribed some medicine to "stop the worm from coiling even more." Carina liked the pills. They numbed her down and made the worm go silent, like she was drunk but in a fuzzier way. What she didn't like so much was that the pills were numbing everything down – she couldn't focus on her work anymore so she had to sleep. Whenever she slept, her dreams got out of control.

That's how she spent her days in Prague. Doing the same thing she did in Amsterdam, only now she had other people to talk to. And they appreciated her work and went out together a couple of times for drinks and dinner at the restaurants around their hotel and all of them were impressed with how much food they could get for only 7.39 euros at a reasonable exchange rate.

They even invited Carina to go out with them and "get wasted," but she would always find some excuse to go to bed before 00:00. In truth, Carina hadn't been to a party in at least six months and eight days, if by party one means getting drunk on two half glasses of wine in room 1914. She didn't like the clubs either – the music was too loud and sex was everywhere. Carina would go to bed at around 23:00, get up at 8:00 sharp, dress up nicely, have a small breakfast, and then go to the student conferences for the rest of the day. Their hotel was in a nice neighbourhood in Prague so they could see all the landmarks, but she didn't. ******

Every day at 8:00 Carina's friend knocked the door to get breakfast together, but today she didn't come. That had never happened before. Instead, two of her colleagues were inexplicably in her room, staring her down as she started to wake up. Carina gasped and asked how had they managed to enter, since she always shut her door at night. She couldn't see them well because she didn't wear glasses, and asked, "Who are you?" sitting half upright in her bed. But her colleagues looked at each other and decided to not answer that question. "I want to see my friend," said Carina, making a movement as if tearing herself away from the two persons. "No," one of the young men said and started looking for her luggage to get some clothes. "We are going to visit Prague together – as a group – and you'd better get dressed. We can't tell you more about this, but you'll learn about everything all in good time." Carina tried to find excuses and even took offense at them walking in like that (what if she had been changing her clothes?) but it didn't help. She still had some work to finish, just some proofreading, no big deal, but her colleagues opened the drawers as if searching for something other than her clothes, threw a pair of jeans and a blouse on her bed, and said "We're meeting downstairs in ten." They were unreasonable and it made Carina uncomfortable. At the back of her mind she couldn't shake the feeling that this was some sort of joke – a complicated prank her new friends were pulling on her. Carina said she would be down in ten.

They walked a lot that day and did all the touristy things. They walked in circles, walked on the Charles Bridge, threw some coins in some street musicians' case who were playing the *String Quartet No. 10 in E flat major Op. 51*, by a guy named Dvořák – one of her colleagues had played the violin since he was five so he knew the song. Carina didn't like it. Like Prague itself, the music was too much.

They walked and walked the streets of the Old Town like some sort of soul-purifying ritual. Carina felt unexpectedly good going out. She laughed and joked with them, they had a nice lunch at one of the terraces near Kafka's statue, took lots of smiling pictures. Her "arrest" from the morning was forgotten. In fact, Carina thanked her colleagues for taking her out and having a good time. She said she needed to unwind after all the work.

They crossed the Charles Bridge one more time at night and took more pictures with the statue of King Charles IV. The bridge became emptier as the day moved through and Carina actually found it enjoyable like this – not crammed with people from four different continents.

It got dark soon. Walking some more, the group heard a loud bass coming from one of the clubs nearby. Immediately drawn in, the guys just disappeared. Carina was taken by her hand and after a quick check from the bouncer, she was in.

The club was nothing special. Loud, bad music, stroboscopic lights that caused epileptic seizures, cigarette smoke, tramps, overpriced drinks, and horny people. Within 20.4 minutes, everyone in her group managed to get a hookup. Everyone but Carina. As time went on and as she tried to dance in a way that wouldn't spill her drink, Carina saw everyone having a good time, everyone was making out with everyone on the tables, on the dance floor, inside cages suspended from the ceiling, there were girls kissing girls – Carina always wanted to see how it was to kiss a girl. Everyone but her. Finishing the rest of her drink and seeing that everyone in her group was too busy to notice her, she left. Outside, a girl was throwing up on the pavement and another one with her makeup ruined held her hair. Across the road, some couples were smoking cigarettes, others were just chatting, and a few more stumbled inside a taxi.

Carina walked back and took a couple of turns on some side streets hoping she would get to her hotel in thirteen minutes rather than twenty-five. But she moved away from all the touristy areas into an alley that didn't have street lights. That type of tight dark alley where bad things happen in the movies. Carina secretly prayed to not get raped while trying to find her way back. Instead she arrived at a house built in the typical Czech baroque style: a couple of pointed towers, a few indistinguishable statues, and a sense of an old European solemnity. Everything was encircled by a metal fence that looked like a bunch of spears stuck in the ground. The gate was particularly beautiful, decorated with cast iron vines that crawled along the spears. Carina didn't know why, but she *had* to enter that house. She knew all the answers she was looking for were there: what she was going to do with her life, how to get back what was stolen, how to be whole again, how to get rid of the worm, is there life after death, *everything*. A few lights went on from the house – the only one on the street – and Carina could see somebody standing in front of the gate. A flap-eared man in a black overcoat and hat.

Carina approached the man, begging admittance to her answers. The man took his hat off and greeted her, revealing a short haircut, the one lawyers would wear. He smiled nervously.

"Is it still open?"

"Yes."

"Can I go in?"

"I don't think so"

"Can I enter at a later time?"

"Maybe later," said the man.

Carina tried to peer through the entrance. Who was in that house? How could she get to talk to the person inside? All her life Carina had been taught that answers should be available to everyone. Her, out of all people.

"You can't go in there," said the lawyer. "I am first in line."

With the man's permission, Carina stood on a bench by the side of the door.

"How long have you been here?"

"Quite some time."

"What's your name?"

"Josef."

"What's inside?"

"The end."

"So how do I get there?"

"You have to wait for me. That's how it works."

"Do you work here?"

"No, I am waiting for the end."

"What if they don't tell you the end?"

"I am just a servant facing the law, Carina, I don't know any of this."

"But the door is open, you can step inside."

"Things don't work that way."

"What if they trick you?"

"If I am not getting in, then you're not getting in."

"But I can't wait forever, I have work to do in the morning."

"Things will sort themselves out. Just wait."

The man put on his hat and clutched the handle of his leather briefcase. On the bench next to him, Carina waited. She took her phone out to tell her friends that she was going to be late at the hotel, but the digits on her watch moved so fast she could barely see them. Was the stopwatch turned on? That was time moving, and Joseph didn't move. Looking at her hands and touching her face, Carina was aging faster than children with progeria. Running out of time but determined to get inside, she gave away everything she had – save for her phone – in the hope of bribing the lawyer, who always said, "I am taking these, but I am first in line. You can't go in before me." Watching herself burning through all the stages of her body, Carina stood on the bench next to the man. "Please, Joseph, I have to get in, what is inside there? The door's open, why don't you go in?" But even when Joseph still said the same thing over again, Carina didn't try to leave, nor did the sun try to appear, and there she was, approaching her death with the numbers on her smartphone running as fast as they could. The lights inside the house where everything ended grew even brighter, making the cast-iron vines look real. Her sight faded, and as she was approaching death, all the questions she had reduced to a single one. Carina questioned Joseph one more time:

"Yes?"

"Why is it that no one else came to wait after me?"

Carina's hearing failed, so the lawyer's voice rose and filled the small streets around the house:

"You know what I always believed?" he said, pronouncing every word individually.

"What?"

"LIFE IS SOMETHING STUPID, AND THEN YOU DIE. And now … there is no point in keeping the door open."

Joseph stepped inside. The iron creaked as it clamped shut. Carina didn't have the strength to get up and follow. She could still hear him as her eyes closed. ******

Carina's therapist said it was the way all stories are born. For now, she woke up in her bed in the hotel in Prague. Her skin wasn't wrinkled anymore. She got out and went by her friend's place at 8:05 to wake her up for breakfast. The plane was in the evening. A guy Carina had not seen before answered the door. He said her friend wasn't there anymore. Thinking of it as another hoax, even bigger than yesterday, Carina went and had breakfast by herself. There was no time to waste.

I decided to block Carina out of my life the moment I saw her pictures from Prague. I had to. All we did was fight and waste time. I was tired of getting shivers in my chest whenever we started stirring each other up. I got lost on all the websites trying to figure out how to block someone. Carina was my first. "It's over," I thought.

I wrote her a couple of messages explaining why I wanted it. Seeing Carina's pictures frustrated me. Seeing her getting better hurt me and I couldn't forgive her for being happy without me. I wanted her to be sad and depressive until I got back, so that she could see me as her only reason to be happy.

How well can you know a person? Something's so rotten about social media. What bothered me most was that Carina was smiling in all her pictures and looked very happy. When we're talking, she tells me how bad and how depressed she is and yet she still finds the ability to fake a smile. I wondered if any of her friends knew the story behind her smile. We want everyone to know how happy we are even when we're not, we post pictures and status changes and pour our feelings out there and nobody cares. Things would be better if we couldn't speak our minds. Seeing those pictures of Carina smiling made me think again about our Cold War or even about a régime like the one in China. You always try to show the better part of yourself to others and hide the things that go wrong. I felt cheated. Why should I be the only one fighting with Carina and the rest of the world see how much fun she's having in Prague? Of course, I couldn't experience the régime on my own, being in Hong Kong, because I'm a foreigner and in a place like this you don't care about these things very much, because you only see the better part of Hong Kong and all its touristy areas and foreigner bars. It's strange how we don't hear about what's going on in that part of the world and all we can do as foreigners is throw a veil over our eyes and continue to have fun and chat up Chinese chicks and of course post some selfies on Facebook. I guess it's easier to say that you don't care about someone else's problems because they are so far away and speak a different language and you have your own stuff to deal with back home.

Carina's ban was double-sided. I hated her Facebook profile, all those updates and pictures, and I hated fighting with her all the time. For the first time in forever, I finally did something good.

The same goes for Fei-yan. Her stories about her past relationships, though fascinating, almost betrayed her as sad and unimportant. Stalking her Facebook profile, I saw she had similar pictures – Colgate smile all the way, looking carefree, always showing her better side. Facebook is a safe haven for depressed people. I cursed myself for attracting a single type of girl – weird. That says something about me in the end. I'm either weird myself (weird people tend to sniff each other out) or I have a strange urge to fix weirdness. Fei-yan started to look at me the way Carina did at the beginning of our relationship – and I was okay with that. It will be almost impossible to have sex, I figured. I had the bad sex for quite some time – after a while, I stopped feeling it, doing it from a sense of inertia, and I have Carina to thank for that. We both lost something somewhere along the way and the intimacy Carina and I shared turned into something else. Sex became a visceral experience. But then she became drier and drier, her world shrank and there was no room for me inside it. We tried and tried, we both wanted to do it (I more than her) but it just died out and she thought I couldn't see it. That's when other problems started appearing. Soon after that we had a silent understanding to not talk about sex. Whenever we would hang out with other people things were great. Worthy of envy, even. But that was only from the outside. Inside, we were trying to find something that was lost on the way to Amsterdam and I was trying to push myself back into her world – and everything was going away the harder we tried.

Dreams of having left and then returning to Hong Kong and meeting Fei-yan again. Most likely it's not going to happen. Too soon to think about leaving. Fool trying to reach some doors that will never open. Carina stood before all of them.

I haven't done any serious school work for more than a month and I didn't feel like it. Spending a lot of money going out drinking and smoking with other Europeans. I missed this decadent nature of mine, like Carina said. The morning-after hangover made me aware of my former teenager-ish self. Carina didn't like to drink.

I went to a party last night. A forest party with a theme: animism. Strange if you think Hong Kong has the exact opposite of an *animus*, a soul. It's hard to believe there are forests in a place like Hong Kong, but once you take a thirty-minute bus ride you find yourself in a place with no electricity, no signs, just a jungle and concrete paths, much like the yellow brick road. So we walked the path for twenty minutes helped by our smart-phones, wondering if we got off at the right stop. The silence around us took the form of a sharp buzzing in our ears, night birds and the rustling wind. The music was getting louder and louder and we came to a clearing where lights hung across the trees and a huge projector showing random fractals (Gandhi was somewhere on the screen too). Around us people were dressed up like animals. Lions, zebras, cats, bears, druids, nymphs, and other creatures danced to the beats of some Hong Kong DJ. We took the bottles of whiskey conveniently stored in our coats and the pills a friendly black man sold to us and started downing it all. The party and the glow-sticks got intense.

I don't know exactly when, but the music melted with the images on the screen and the glow sticks turned into souls, sprites of life thrown from one end of the clearing to another. An hour or so in, I saw the lion kissing the zebra on the neck but my mind was already jumping to the circle of life. The druids took some nymphs away and dragged them into the trees nearby, the bear chugged vodka like water in a corner and the projections made us believe we have but a small part to play in this world, that we are small and insignificant and should connect with the greater forces that dictate our fate as if we are their test subjects.

A friend of mine reached for his backpack and pulled out a long scarf with some Middle Eastern patterns and threw it over the people. The way the scarf moved below us looked like we were under water and light bullets of green, red and blue pierced it from time to time. A girl who looked like a cat started dancing next to me. She asked me if I wanted to taste something darker than the swoon of sin and tried to kiss me. I kissed her right back. In that moment of complete abandonment there was hardly anything else around me other than the dark pressure of her softly parting lips. The way she did it, it felt like she was kissing my brain rather than my lips and I heard us talking at a level that went beyond two people exchanging saliva. I looked around and there were other people kissing under the scarf, huddling together as if trying to avoid the rays of light.

It was becoming hard to breathe. People kept coming and coming and before long the clearing became overcrowded, just like the rest of Hong Kong. I had a designer shirt and a tailored blazer on me, which is, in a way, a form of animism in itself. I had been hoping to meet Fei-yan in town but in the end she stood me up. An Austrian girl asked me if I wasn't Dutch, because "Everything about you is so Dutch! I had a guy who was from Rotterdam and you remind me of him!" It wasn't long before other people start noticing me. The lion, tired from biting the zebra's neck, started walking around the clearing, checking out the dancing under the scarf. Seeing me, he yelled and pointed in my direction and started bowing in front of me, hands gripping his staff in front of him and mumbling something in a language I couldn't understand. Others started following his example and before long, all the people in the clearing started bowing in front of me and my blazer. There was a half-metre circle between me and the worshipers. The beats changed and the whole party started a strange dance as if they were shamans dancing around the fire. The lights dimmed and my black blazer started to glow the harder the people danced. Its glow was so bright that it started burning. I felt ashamed standing there as if I'd wet myself in front of the class so I took off my blazer and ran away into the crowd. After the party I wanted to go back and take my blazer back, but everyone I asked said they couldn't remember anything. When I saw the pictures from the party, there was a patch of grass that was scorched and it looked slightly like a piece of clothing.

There were so many people dancing that it stopped being enjoyable. I left and I couldn't remember where my blazer was. The dancing went on. There were some benches by the clearing so I went there. At least the air was breathable. On one end of the bench there were two English girls making out with each other. They didn't seem to be bothered by me. In front, there was this American guy wearing a Miami Heat jersey and he was so wasted he couldn't lift his head from the dirt. He was on his knees with his head down. People were passing by him barely noticing. He would've fallen down anyway if I'd helped him. At least he wasn't hurting anybody this way. A guy sat uncomfortably close to me. He took a cigarette out and asked me if I smoked. I said, "Sure," and took one from his pack. He lit it for me and we both sat there on the bench saying nothing. The music stopped for a couple of minutes so we could better hear the English girls moan while making out on the same bench and touching each other. The guy finished his cigarette, squished it under his boot and left into the night. "I'll never see that man again, I thought."

It took twenty-five minutes to gather all the people from my group who wanted to go back home. We walked the concrete path back to the city. Hong Kong Island was incredibly quiet. The lights from all the shops and commercials were off, barely any taxis on the road, taking some lost tourists to their hotels, and several dim sum places opening up for their elderly clientèle who would be coming in soon. We stopped at one of those places, pointing at pictures of food we wanted to eat. Then we walked the streets some more, treading very carefully, as if not wanting to wake up a sleeping dragon. We took the famous Hong Kong tram and everything felt like in a movie from the 1950s. If a girl in a ballroom dress with pearl earrings and hair made up to look like a scorpion's tail had stepped into the tram (but girls like that don't take the tram, let's be serious), I wouldn't have been surprised.

On our way back we wanted to see the sunrise, but it got cloudy. By the time I arrived at the dorms, I saw the guard sleeping and I scared him. I had to apologize and the seconds it took until the elevator came were unbearable for the both of us. I went to bed without changing my clothes. I can be happy too and post pictures about it so my friends die of envy. I wondered what Fei-yan was doing. Hollowness tucked me in. It was one of those nights in Hong Kong when you start thinking about them long after they have passed.

Carina's therapist encouraged her to do a couple of things.
1.   She should go out of the house more and take care of herself.
2. Minimize contact with me as much as possible.
3. If there was any contact, she should not back down.

Carina returned to Amsterdam from Prague. She waited for her luggage at conveyor belt 9 and she stepped out at Arrivals 2. There were lots of people – waiting for other people. The sight made Carina free. Every time she flew somewhere there was someone waiting for her at Arrivals 2 – family, friends, even me. But this time, all the people were waiting for someone else. She secretly hoped that someone, anyone, would be there for her and she even walked around dragging her suitcase, trying to see if anybody just around the corner or reading a newspaper on a bench had missed her. Carina's group booked their flights a day later so she was by herself. Carina stood in front of the arrivals hall for a moment longer. She wasn't sure all this sudden freedom brought something good. Still, she managed her way through the airport and jumped on the train back to her place – back to Solitude.

I suggested to Carina that she visit me in Hong Kong, but she was very upset at the thought of just "visiting." She didn't want her "just visiting" status to be rubbed in by the little taste only that I could give her of what to me had become my daily life. She would take this time to think about what she wants: Who knew, Carina, you would have found something nice trying to give yourself an answer. After all, she promised me she would be happy. The numbers were slowly losing their meaning. She stopped counting the times she needed to rub the shampoo and the seconds it needed to act, she stopped counting the dishes, she didn't even check the temperature every hour. Prague wasn't so bad. It wasn't Hong Kong, but still.

This weekend, Amsterdam was unusually sunny and warm. Carina decided to take her therapist's advice and go somewhere in town. She packed a blanket and biked towards the Museumplein by herself. Solitude waved goodbye and locked the door.

The ground was cold, but that didn't stop Carina from lying down on the blanket, even for fifteen minutes. The sun put

Carina in a good mood, and for the first time, she was optimistic. Other people were on the grass too. Some were throwing frisbees to their dogs while others were throwing a ball to each other. Kids were flying a kite somewhere in the background. A bunch of tourists gathered in front of the Rijksmuseum. A girl passed by and mumbled to her boyfriend that there were too many tourists for her to take a picture.

From her blanket, Carina could see some bikes and some scooters waiting at the traffic lights. There were nine rows of three bikes each and two scooters. The way they were arranged, Carina imagined the bikes were like a herd of sheep and the scooters like shepherds. Lying on her blanket, thinking about life like a true grown-up. Dutch bikes waiting at the traffic light. Carina's ambitions melted away for one second. Those seconds, expanded indefinitely, made Carina never want to leave her blanket. Or maybe – she could take her bike and ride along the "bike herd" to an unknown part of the city, led away by some scooters along the bike lane. But before she could make a move, the light turned green and everyone whizzed past the cross-roads. It was only then she felt it. Her ovaries were sensitive and she feared she could catch a cold. Carina's mom always told her not to sit on cold surfaces otherwise her tummy would hurt. She stood up, fixed her clothes, packed the blanket and left.

On her way back, Carina was already feeling better about herself. When she got home, Solitude waved, but she couldn't be bothered to wave back. Just like the first time, Carina, if you'd ignore Solitude, then it might leave. She took a long shower, shaved her legs just to kill time and made a simple dinner. She had begun to eat healthier since I left.

Carina decided to go to bed early so that her good mood would continue the next morning. She picked a book and snuggled into bed. She didn't even check the messages on her phone. Going to the therapist was a good decision, wasn't it, Carina? All her life she thought she could solve her problems on her own – even this one. So far, everything worked.

People *need* people other than using them to achieve your own purpose. She didn't understand this, and it would take some time before Carina would apply this principle in real life. Like maths. You needed some practice before you could understand a theorem. Her thoughts seemed to return to that moment on the blanket where she saw the bikes packed up like a herd at the traffic light. She knew it had a certain significance but it was impossible for her to explain it in words or even understand it completely. How several seconds turned into what seemed like years. Sometimes time can dilate like that in Europe, especially on a sunny day in Amsterdam. Sometimes, a whole life can go by in several seconds, more likely to happen on a crazy night in Prague. Maybe she should give up on her ambitions and enjoy "the moment"? Her therapist told her that she probably aimed too high – planning for a thing for so long like she did for Hong Kong and then having to change it in a matter of days had triggered her "condition." It was just like in the poem she read, with the kitchen-sink falling in love with a yellow star – we all knew that sinks cannot be in love with stars. Maybe it was just destiny's hand, maybe she wasn't supposed to go and other forces had decided it in advance. – Carina was reminded of her grandma trying to make her feel better. – Maybe the kitchen sink asked for too much, falling in love with the star. Maybe I wasn't so guilty after all for going abroad – but that didn't mean I was less guilty. Love is one thing, robbing someone is another.

Carina put the book aside. Her thoughts after just three therapy sessions of precisely forty-five minutes each made it too much to handle for one of the many single nights that were to come. The time was 22:33. The temperature inside the room was twenty-three degrees Celsius. Solitude slept on the floor that night.

listen, i just wanted to let you know that if you have anything
else left to say, you can write me an e-mail
don't hate me for it
but just the fact that i'm seeing you online here puts me in a
place i don't want to be
i just don't want to hear from you for a while
i don't care what's going to happen or what isn't
but now for me you are something i don't associate with a nice
thing
i'm glad that you promised me you're going to feel better
you should
you deserve it
i'm sorry so many things piled on top of you right now and i feel
bad about it
but there's nothing i can do about it
you can throw away the things i have in your room but please
keep the books i liked the mst
most*
i'm sorry they make you think of me but believe it or not
i also have some things from you with me that make me think of
our days in amsterdam
and our strange relationship
you know, that relationship held together by the objects we've
been giving to each other
gifts you actually never wanted
but don't worry
a gift is still a gift no matter what
i just hope that you'll reach the moment where you see a thing
that makes you think of me
be just a memory like a bad dream that can be chased away
because things are alright in hong kong with the guy that wasn't
supposed to go in the first place
and they will be good even when i come back to ams
i know many things could have been avoided if i didn't
encourage you to come and study in Amsterdam
and i know this is not the place you want to be right now
funny how some things come in line, i know
but all i wish for you is to be happy
i was too small and too stupid to believe i could give you such a

thing
i think these are the things i wanted to say to you
and maybe these are the things left unsaid between us
at least the way i see it
because it would be something stupid to imagine a relationship
with you right now
just like you said, we're better off.
funny how i managed to get the balls to actually do this right
now
never actually imagined how it would be like to give up on you
it's like cutting off a diseased hand
i have to cut it off to live
but it's something important to me at the same time
never mind the metaphors.
i hope you're going to be happy; i really wish it and i say it
without any sarcasm or irony (you know, the way we've been
used to for this whole time)
take care
try to connect the dots
you're a smart young woman, you'll understand ******

Subject: RE: Fb message

Im going to answer one thing at a time. Im actually
struggling to type it properly. My keyboard is
broken so I cant use the apostrophe.

1.   It doesnt matter. The only thing that
mattered was to get back to you after you said you
regret those 4 euros you paid for the flowers and
candy on the 14th of February – which, btw, it's a
very nasty thing to say.

2.   I dont think we had a fake relationship for
2 years. If thats what you understood that our
relationship was about buying things for each other,
youre wrong.

3.   Ill never get to look at something you gave me and see the way you were trying to keep me close to you. Just so you know, Im saying oh, that time i was with my boyfriend or my boyfriend said this and that AT LEAST once a day. And theyre never bad things, theyre just things inside me.

4.   I have no intention of getting back to you in any way. I respect you a lot and I respect our relationship. It would be common sense to talk to each other once youll be back. I dont know if you realize it and I know our conversatiions werent the best, but I MISS U. After all this time together I cant just get over you in two months. I hope thats true for u as well.

5.   Its not very nice to say u were too stupid to give me happiness. I think we shouldve given happiness to ourselves.

As far as Im concerned:

I dont want to stop talking to u. Weve known each other for 6 years now. Its just stupid. Id understand if we were back in our country, but come on, things are different here. And weve shared too much to just kick it away just like that. Maybe now it's a good moment for both of us to step back and figure thing out. Its an IMPORTANT stage in both of our lives, maybe even more important to you because youre out there. There is so much to work with ourselves before anything else. Who knows whats going to happen when youre back? There is no certainty in my life, not even for a couple of days.

Ive been very affected by your departure. I thought Ill never make it on my own. ALL MY LIFE Ive been depending on my parents and gradually on you. Every time I came back from school I knew you were home waiting for me and I couldnt wait to jump in bed with u and snuggle. In the beginning, I was very sad whenever I came home because I knew you weren't there for me. I thought Ill never be able to replace that joy of coming back home. But now Ive learned to accept it and now Im happy to go back home because Ill have some nice food. Dont think I replaced the joy of seeing you with eating.

I reached a point where I never was: perfectly alone. I dont know how its going to be, but Im trying to make the most out of it and understand its magic. Its hard, but Im sure its hard for you out there as well. From what Ive heard, most of the students who go to the end of the world get depressed. I hope its not that way with you. Youve been given this amazing opportunity to be there, its a blessing in my opinion. I hope you take advantage of this, just like you said you did and do all the things you couldnt do because of me. Which is strange because you spent that much time with me and yet you said I was holding you back and you liked it. Now you can be 17 over again. I think its fun.

I wish for you to be happy and dont hold any grudges. I wont hold anything (just your stuff) and I wish we could say hello to each other when we bump into each other on the street.

I dont see our break up as something final. I see it as a different stage in our lives right now. You dont know where life is going to take us along the way. And now, as we are at 9277.76 kilometers away from each other we can stand on our own 2 legs. You can do the things youve always wanted to do and I can learn to finally be independent.
        Message sent 9:41 AM.

I've decided I'm not going to work myself too hard. As Carina said, being in Hong Kong was a once in a lifetime opportunity. I can study harder when I get back to Amsterdam. For now, I had to cherish and live every single moment of this city.

I missed hiking. The only hiking you can do in the Netherlands is when you climb the dunes to see the seaside and that's about it. Hong Kong was surrounded by mountains and forests, many of which were open for hiking and trekking. A group was going on a hike and I decided to join in. I woke up very late so I didn't have time to pack much. At 15:00 I was in front of the railway station. We waited for a while longer for the people who were late and left. We took the train for two stations, then changed for a 45-minute bus ride. I couldn't believe how the city changed once you got out in the surrounding areas. The tower-blocks were giving way to the large trees, the roads became smaller, the cars and people fewer and fewer. Getting down off the bus meant stepping into a completely different world, one that looked more like a poor village. The monster called Hong Kong was not around anymore. It was strange to witness, since the city sank its teeth so deep into your neck that you couldn't see or hear anything else. It was hard to believe there was room for nature and green spaces in Hong Kong.

The trail was made of giant concrete slabs pasted together, and it reminded me of the party in the forest. I heard one of the group members saying it looked like the yellow brick road from the Wizard of Oz. He wasn't too far from the truth. Even here, surrounded by nature, everything was preordained, pretty much like every experience for a foreigner visiting Hong Kong. The slabs (probably the same ones I walked on a couple of days ago) were a giant claw mark left by the city in the middle of the forest. A bit like Buddhist monks with smartphones. Even here, you would only get an *impression* of what being "in nature" meant. Praising the trees and the fresh air could only be made standing on the concrete, this couldn't be done without praising man with every step you took for his achievements in bending nature to his will. We started following the trail and the sun almost hid behind a mountain.

The hike ended on a beach after we walked for a couple of

hours. It got dark soon, but there were lights every ten metres with a sign that always pointed forward, as if there was another direction. The backpacks, lanterns, and the ridiculous uniforms the other people had were pointless from the beginning. I have never seen a mountain that opened up onto a beach. The gulf and beach was about 100 metres long. From the top, the rocks that encompassed the beach and the gulf looked like the claws of a giant stone crab. It was dark by the time we got there and the last leg of the hike was scary – we barely had any light to go by. We rented some tents at the conveniently placed boutique by the end of the trail and set them on the beach. Everyone was tired after the long hike and one by one they went to sleep. I had to share my tent with two other people, but because I didn't pack a sleeping-bag, I couldn't sleep. It wasn't windy at all, but the sand was cold and the layer between my clothes and tent thin. I put on my other shirt that I had with me but that did not help.

What was even worse was that I could not stop thinking. Thoughts can be crippling sometimes and even though I wanted sleep, my mind was racing as if I had downed five espressos.

I got out of the tent and walked outside onto the beach. I sat there for a while by myself. Maybe if I turned away from the lights of the boutique and walked along the beach in darkness I would take my mind off Carina and Fei-yan. There was absolutely no wind coming in from the sea. Very close to the shore, there were some fluorescent algae or plankton washed up by the waves. On the wet sand, they looked like a fireworks show seen from a distance. The shores kept the contours of the weeds and then they rolled back once the waters pulled back. But then, as the waves brought more and more, I could see the contour of Carina's face in the wet sand of the beach. As the waters moved back and forth, it seemed like she was saying something or that she was happy. A few steps to the right, I made out Fei-yan's features.

Just like in those very old movies, where you have to turn a crank to watch things happen frame by frame, I watched Carina's and Fei-yan's faces turning into roses. They were a shade of green that looked almost like blue, and they lit that part of the beach each time the waves turned back. But then the roses moved slowly towards each other, were superimposed for a brief moment, and got splashed onto the sand. I went back to my tent and waited for the sun to come up. As the first light hit the ground, I started going back to campus. I tried to tell some other people what I saw last night, but they said I was hallucinating from not sleeping.

"Maybe every man has had two such women – at least two." The story with the red rose and white rose. Where are my roses? Someone was choking me, someone was showing me signs I was supposed to make sense of. I had to make a choice and time was running out. Love as time. I don't know how I got home by myself. Hollowness was more than happy to take care of my dreams and memories, and when it saw what I did, there was no way those images would come back to me again.

The room felt like someone had just been there. The old shirt Solitude wore got soaked in my smell as the days went on and because Carina was still trying to figure out what happened in Prague, she did little to notice it. Too many things were happening. Since I left, new worlds were opening in front of Carina once every two days and she was not ready for that. Freedom is a difficult thing to work with, especially if it's given to you all of the sudden. Carina didn't think I was taking away her freedom too much, but you knew how it was, Carina, you had to make some compromises in a relationship. Everywhere she looked, people were making decisions for her in one way or another. What she wanted, what she was looking for, was out of reach somehow, and after a while, one tends to quit. And because you quit, you let others do the decisions for you. On the outside, Carina looked like a strong young woman. In her previous relationship, she made most of the decisions because her boyfriend couldn't make them or didn't want to have anything to do with choices. But all the choices she made were superficial: where to go out tonight, what to eat for dinner, what to do on vacation, things like that. Her boyfriend never objected to anything, and she was alright with that. All those small decisions counted for nothing because *now* she could do whatever she wanted. For now, Carina decided she would order some sushi and go to sleep. Carina didn't like sushi that much, especially since one day she saw some mice in her favourite sushi bar. That day, two policemen were patrolling and in all seriousness, she said there were mice inside the sushi bar. Trying not to laugh, the policemen said that dealing with mice is not in their power and she'd better call the customer service office or something like that. They must've thought she was high or something. But this sushi day was special. Like the mice, she could roam around the restaurant, stealing fish and rice because the customers and the sushi master were all gone. Carina showered until the food came. Solitude pulled out a pair of chopsticks once the food arrived and knelt next to the small table. The sushi wasn't so bad, she liked the salmon one the most. Everything went down with some beer, and afterwards they pulled the curtains and snuggled into bed.

Carina's friends from Prague came to see her the day after,

not feeling like the party was over. They talked to Carina, said they're going to shower, take a nap, and then go out again. It would be a shame if she didn't join in, they said.

Carina was free now. And even though she wasn't a fan of clubs and wanted to stay in and read a nice book (if there ever was a thing in common between Carina and me it was definitely our hate for nightclubs), she chose, as a free young woman, to join without too much convincing on the part of her friends. She took some time off her regular routine to dress up and put on make-up. When the time came, she took her bike from the bike shed and met the new-found friends just outside the building.

As they got there, they were checked by a menacing-looking bald bodyguard in a black suit and white tie. They handed in their coats to be looked after for the small sum of two euros, and then in they were.

The music was loud, and Carina could feel the loud bass in her stomach and toes. People were dancing everywhere – middle-aged women with slutty skirts were climbing onto the bar; on her right, some morbidly obese girls were downing Jägerbombs while yelling "Wooooooooo!" as loud as they could. Other people were taking selfies with the DJ and the stroboscopic lights made Carina dizzy. Crowds of people poured in and started dancing to the same beats you'd find in any club. It's a shame we like the same things over and over again. Carina tried to close her eyes so that she wouldn't trip because of the daze, but then again, there were so many sweaty people in the club someone might push her into a table or the bar if she wasn't careful. Standing against the bar, she could see up underneath the middle-aged women's skirts – one of them had a tampon that definitely needed to be changed. Filled with disgust, Carina tried to imagine what would happen if one of those women's kids – if they had any – were to walk right onto the dance floor watching his/her mom humiliating herself like that on top of the bar of a club in Amsterdam's Leidseplein. But then again, Carina thought, that baby must've been dumped in a toilet or wrapped in a plastic bag and thrown in a nearby dumpster in a crappy community college twenty years ago.

Amid all this, three of Carina's friends yelled in her ear that four Jägerbombs cost only ten euros. Maybe that was the key to enjoy this mess – getting drunk. As a newly-free young woman,

Carina bought the first round. Yelling, but barely covering the sound of music, the girls went straight for the bar and Carina slammed a ten-euro bill on the table. She yelled to the bartender she wanted four (what was that again?) Jägerbombs. After much spinning and juggling of the bottles and cans, the bartender seemed to be wrapped in a light show that was sent by God himself. The bartender put five small beer glasses on the bar. One was empty; the others had Red Bull. Then he rested the shot glasses in the space between the larger ones. He tipped the first shot glass, triggering a domino effect. The Jägerbombs were ready. Carina's friends yelled in excitement but she could barely hear them; the music and the lights and the noise was too loud for anything. The girls cheered and started racing towards the bottom of the glass. Carina didn't like the drink, and after her first sip she wanted to put the glass down. But one of her friends, as though reading her mind, placed her finger at the bottom of Carina's glass and her eyes and eyebrows made a gesture that said "Up! Up!" and slowly pushed the glass. Carina coughed after she was done, and she gave a nasty look at her friend. "That's how you drink Jägerbombs, Carina! All at once!" The drink wasn't too strong, but it made Carina feel warm on the inside. Just like in the beginning, Carina's friends melted away in that mass of bodies and noise. Slowly, the music moved Carina. She began to dance slowly at first, and gradually, she was drawn to the mass of people, of decadent and depraved people. Her moves, clumsy and stiff, were imitations of other young women who believed these kinds of displays of sexuality made them feel empowered and sexy. Carina felt neither empowered nor sexy. Just tipsy. As she danced, a guy came closer to her. Soon, he was dancing next to her. He approached her from the side, so that she could see him coming with the back of her eyes. Carina couldn't distinguish his features clearly (who could in these lights?) but she was on her guard when the guy pushed her hair from her ear back to her neck and said:

"Hi, I'm Jan."

I could barely make Fei-yan come down and have lunch with me. Since that night, I would wait for her downstairs to go and have our lunch together, but she never showed up. The minutes passed from five to ten to fifteen to twenty, and the elevator refused to climb up to the girls' floors, leaving me stuck with the guard and the passers-by, who were smiling to me as if they knew something I didn't. Texting, calling, Facebook, nothing worked. I tried going to her room a couple of times but all the pretexts that I could come up with were pathetic, so I quit. A few days had already passed and I couldn't shake the feeling that something was out of place, like a fortress the night before the siege.

Eventually, Fei-yan texted me, "Lunch? Downstairs in ten," after God knows how long. I threw some clothes on and in five minutes was waiting for her in the lobby. The lift went up to her floor then down again. In it, Fei-yan. Her eyes, full with the things she wanted to say but couldn't, and her hair wet, I could not speak. I knew nothing. Looking into the heart of light that came outside the elevator, I was greeted by silence and crossed arms.

We didn't talk. She walked past me straight to the front doors. She was shorter than me, but I had to struggle to keep up with her as we were walking down to the canteen. Still, complete silence. The term to describe a foreigner in Cantonese is literally translated as "ghost man." It was like I was hanging around her like a bad spirit or more like a bad omen. I was almost running to keep up with her. Whenever I caught up with Fei-yan and saw a glimpse of her face, there was a barely perceptible smile, a kind of sarcasm that you couldn't believe a face as pretty as hers was able to put on. What was wrong with me whenever I was around this girl, this girl whom I could never love, this girl whom I would never see again in my life?

We didn't talk. We arrived at the canteen and Fei-yan looked on the menu and ordered in Chinese. I did the same thing right after her and sat at a table that she picked. All this time, she was looking at her phone, she was checking her Facebook and chatting with some faceless and nameless people. Some other guys came to her and started talking in Chinese. Her face would open up in that smile I was familiar with, but as soon as they left, things were back the way they were before. She raised her eyes from her phone a couple of times to see my reaction. It was like we were playing a game of chicken. Who would give up first? How much could I took before I'd press the button that launched the nuclear warheads?

Looking around the large hall, I noticed the place was really noisy. I ate there almost every day but this was the first time I heard how noisy it was. Cutlery smashing against the bowls, chairs grinding on the floor, students chatting and laughing in a language I could not speak, static tones coming from the huge speakers, the buzzing of the coffee machines, the meat cleaver chopping up ducks and chickens and pigs with metronomic precision, the "ding!" sound whenever the takeaway was ready, the sound of a Chinese woman shouting orders to the kitchen staff. But with all this noise around me my ears heard a sharp buzz like the one you have when you step into a very silent room. It was so sharp I could barely stand it.

Fei-yan was proud. Every once in a while she would put on a mean smile and look in my direction while talking to some other people. I wondered what she was thinking about me, what kind of person was behind that smile, which changed faster than I can sketch it in here. If you looked at her from the side, there was something about her eyes and lips that seemed to stage a coup to the overall prettiness of her face, but there were some days when she looked at me and I could only convince my vocal cords to say "Yes!" to her every request. I still have the pictures she sent me the day I left Hong Kong and I can't recognize her in any of them. This magic of hers worked only in close-range.

"Why don't you want to tell me you don't like it when we don't talk?" Fei-yan asked all of the sudden.

Finally, she could see the ghosts.

"I don't know what to say."

"I dropped my phone and cracked the screen. Do you know what that means?"

"What?"

"I will have a very big fight with somebody. Every single time I break my screen, I fight with someone."

"Me?"

"Not you. You gave me a reason."

Both of us had nothing on our plates.

"Stay here. I will be back," she said.

Fei-yan was back five minutes later with another tray. There was a cup of coffee and tea with some French toast on top of it.

"No milk and a bit of sugar."

I thanked her for the treat. A few moments of silence followed. Plenty of time to admire the noise around.

"You touched my bed."

"Did I?"

"Do not lie to me. I had to change the sheets that night. You crumpled my duvet and messed my pillow. I smelled your hands on my bed. Nobody touches my bed."

"I'm sorry."

"I told you. I told you not to do it and you did it. You are very lucky I am talking to you right now. If I did not make such a fuss over it maybe you would not have done it. But you can never step into my room again. That is the price you have to pay. I trusted you and you betrayed me. Very lucky I am talking to you right now."

There was a chance.

"What's wrong with your bed?"

"Why do you ask so many questions?"

"Asking questions relaxes me."

"I have forgiven you already and we had lunch together. What do you mean, things are tense?"

"Never mind."

Moment of silence. Fei-yan was barely moving her lips as if she was rehearsing some lines before a performance.

"Have you been to the cinema before?"

"Here? No."

"Come to the cinema with me. We can watch something. Things will not be so tense afterwards. Meet me in an hour in front of the dorms."

After some small talk, we left for our rooms in complete silence. Even though most of the people who had lunch had left, the canteen was still just as noisy. ******

"Heat. This is what cities mean to me," I remember reading it in a book once. You don't get that much heat in Amsterdam, since it rains all the time, but in a city like Hong Kong, you feel the heat as soon as you exit the air-conditioned buildings. I waited for Fei-yan in the lobby as usual. The same heart of light came out the elevator along with Fei-yan. She was in a yellow skirt with diamond-like patterns and a white blouse. The blouse didn't have a low-cut neck, but the upper part was almost transparent, barely showing the lace of her bra.

Again. Heat. That is what cities mean to me. We felt the gush of hot air as we got out of the train at Tsim Sha Tsui station. The faceless and nameless people pouring in and out of the crowds rubbing against each other creating friction, gigantic blowers howling to cool people off. The heat radiating from the tall buildings and the neon lights from all the advertisements. The sweat of black people or Pakistanis trying to sell you soft drugs, tailored suits, and fake watches, the heat of the cars and our breath. It was the same heat that melted us into a single crowd, two people trying to walk on the same line without having two or three more around us. Fei-yan was the molecule I had to connect with if I was to survive in this melting pot. Watching her yellow skirt and white blouse navigating through the crowds became my sole purpose the moment I stepped on the platform. I got close to her at some point and touched her hand for no reason. It made me safe knowing that she was there with me.

"Do you like holding hands?" I said to her dodging the people.

"With whom? You?"

"No, not with me. Do tell if you have a boyfriend."

"Yes, I would not mind. But not in public."

"I like holding hands. It's harder to get lost out there."

Another wave of people. Another announcement in Cantonese, Mandarin, and then English.

"Are you hitting on me?"

"Maybe."

The mall where we were supposed to watch the movie was built in such a way that there was a guarantee of getting lost. Good marketing strategy, I thought. Shops I never heard of with prices that will remain forever inaccessible to me. Chandeliers, fountains, stairs that imitated marble, palm trees and the sound of water dropping, Chopin playing on the speakers in the main court, the smell of leather from major clothing chains, perfumes from major Italian designers, golden reflecting surfaces and escalators everywhere. Wealthy Chinese people were having their bags filled with some brands that I can't even remember but nonetheless ridiculously expensive, there were people swearing allegiance to one chain of stores or another without a particular reason, people having the veil of well-being and prosperity pulled over their eyes. Walking around, there was always *another* shop, another café, another alternative to everything. I was even more uncomfortable walking along the mall with Fei-yan, who was being watched by those rich Chinese with their wives and/or mistresses by the arm. "It works wonders for my self-esteem," she said. "Knowing that people want you is one of the best feelings you can have."

We managed to get to the cinema in the end. I didn't remember what the movie was about, and even if I did, it would be pointless to talk about it here. Fei-yan and I went to watch something so that my profanity for touching her bed would be forgotten. And so we did. We talked about the movie for five minutes or so, irrelevant things. Unlike at lunch time, Fei-yan's expression softened, welcoming me with the smile I was used to.

"Follow me. Let's get some dinner."

We were again thrown into that world of luxury, perfume, gold mirrors, heat and sweat.

"Where do you want to eat?"

"I don't know, it's your city. How about this Japanese restaurant?"

"I do not quite enjoy eating at a Japanese restaurant, but since you are the guest, I can make an exception."

"But..."

"Come on."

I couldn't say no. She looked at me again in that manner I could not say no to. We took an elevator filled with old people to the third floor. The waiter pointed us to a table and we sat there. Even though the place was warmly lit and the windows had nice decorations in red and white that blocked the light, we were still standing on the same level with a gigantic pink and green Chinese character. Traditional Japanese music was on the speakers. The tables were lined up like in a diner and on the other side a miniature Japanese garden.

"When my parents first visited me in Hong Kong we had dinner at this place. I do not know why, we do not quite enjoy Japanese food. I think it was raining that day."

We ordered some sushi, salad with sesame sauce dressing and some rice with *tonkatsu*.

"Thank you. There aren't many Japanese restaurants in Amsterdam. My ex-girlfriend once saw some mice in a sushi bar. And then she went to some policemen outside telling them there were mice inside. They struggled not to laugh at her. I did. I laughed all the way back home and then some few days after."

It made her smile.

"That was silly.... Why weren't you more definite that you wanted to come here, in the first place?"

"Because it's nice and polite to go to places that both of us would enjoy."

"I can come here whenever I want with whoever I want. I am being nice to you now."

"That's why I said thanks."

"Why are there so many Westerners in Japanese restaurants? I always wondered what is the thing with Japan and the West? Why not China and the West?"

"Well, there is China and the West too. Maybe Westerners like Japan because it's weird. It's different. And then there are the samurai, the ninja, and all that other cool stuff."

"Do you think I am weird?"

"No, no," I said almost instantly. "Well, I don't know. It's too soon to tell."

"But I do not like it when people touch my bed. Is that not weird?

"Maybe, but it's not enough."

"Yes, it is."

The conversation was becoming more uncomfortable by the second. Luckily, the food came. It was a lot.

"Do you think we'll be able to finish everything?"

"Yes. Food makes me happy," she said.

"But you don't seem to show any signs of prosperity."

"I do not get fat."

She frowned.

I was becoming more and more skillful with chopsticks. I refused to eat with them not because all foreigners did it but because it felt like a mindless form of imitation. The gates of Asia would not open themselves to me because I could bring food to my mouth with chopsticks. But in this case I was too embarrassed to ask for a fork and knife and tried not to make a fool of myself. So far, the chopsticks-to-mouth ratio was good and my clothes were spared. Fei-yan was eating in silence with that same lost grace. It was hard for me to believe how someone her size could eat like that. Before long, the table was cleared. The calm Japanese music contrasted with the speed we ate. Once that was fast-forwarded, time seemed to slow down to the pace of the *koto*.

"Do you like chocolate?"

"Sure, why not."

Fei-yan waved to the waiter and spoke in Chinese. After a short while, we had our Royce' chocolates on a coffee plate. She took the small fork and placed its tip in the praline. There was a barely perceivable trace of chocolate mixed with her lipstick. She then took a napkin and wiped it off. Her eyes, once made to look inside the human soul, were now like the golden reflecting surfaces in the mall. There were two more pralines left and she gestured with her hand for me to eat them.

"Good food makes me happy. It is hard to get good food in China. You learn to appreciate good food in time, even if it is Japanese."

We split the bill and walked out in the heat of Hong Kong. Fei-yan said she wasn't ready to go back to the campus and suggested we take a walk down the Avenue of Stars. Seeing Fei-yan walk, it was hard not to notice how often she tripped and stumbled for no particular reason. Sometimes when she had water she would spill it on the corners of her lips and how could I have forgotten that time when she spilled all her orange juice on her pants? It was like her grace had seizures from time to time but just like her eating, it didn't take away from her overall charm, not at all. When I asked her how come she trips that much she replied "Doesn't it make you want to help me?" She was right. But maybe that that wasn't her intention after all.

The Avenue of Stars. Tourists, live performances, indistinct chatter, a statue with a film strip running around her and a globe of light on top, people trying to document every single moment of their lives and every single moment of what was going on around them. Professional photographers with cheap-looking tripods asking you to have your photo taken against the iconic Hong Kong skyline that looked like a movie décor or a giant coloured panel made out of cardboard. The pavement was filled with the names of people I couldn't read or didn't know, nicely lined up on identical-looking stars set ten metres apart. In the distance, a crowd was gathered in front of what it looked like a statue of a Chinese man. "That is Bruce Lee," Fei-yan said. "And look, there is my favourite building, the Bank of China. And that is the tallest building in Hong Kong, the IFC Tower." The light show of the corporations, banks, international organizations, governmental buildings, finance centres, headquarters of firms and clothing brands, the apartment towers and the houses of the rich somewhere at the back showed their logos, projected lights, their power, their space, their share of Hong Kong Island.

"You're like a terminally diseased patient. You and this place around you will be dead in a couple of months. How do you think you're going to be then? I'll tell you. You're gonna be just like that time when you left. That girl next to you? Oh yeah, she's gonna help you feel like shit. Best part is, you're not gonna see her again. Go on, talk to her, get the feels for her. You're hollow and you don't even know it."

We sat on the railing in a place where it seemed there were fewer tourists. Fei-yan asked me what was wrong but I didn't want to say. If you looked at our faces, the way they turned red, blue, green, yellow, and our amazement in front of the drawn cardboard on the night sky, you could say we were watching fireworks. The water separating Tsim Sha Tsui from Hong Kong Island was calm. A few junks passed by.

"Tell me a story," Fei-yan said coming next to me.

"I'm not sure I can tell a story. Some people have a gift for telling stories."

She was disappointed. Looking at my bony shoulder, Fei-yan carried a fight inside her. Could she rest her head there? Would it be weird? In the end she gave up.

"What are you thinking?"

"If you take the skyscrapers away and make the boats look a bit different, it looks like Amsterdam."

"This is not Amsterdam. This is Hong Kong. Why do foreigners like to talk about their home so much all the time?"

"I thought Amsterdam was my home, but it wasn't. Have you seen *The Lord of the Rings*? There is a scene where the fat guy Sam says to Frodo, 'If I take one more step, I'll be the farthest away from home I've ever been.' I am pretty far. This is just my way of coping with things. If I say this thing looks like Amsterdam or that place looks like home, then it's not so bad."

"What is home to you now?"

"Amsterdam? Hong Kong? The people? Or is it a feeling that you get when you say, 'I'm home'?"

"It is just a combination of these things. I traveled a lot. There are pieces of me everywhere. My hometown, Singapore, Hong Kong, even in Europe I left something. All these places I have been to, they are just the rooms in my house and they are rooms where different people live. In some rooms I like to go more than the others. Now I am in Hong Kong, the worst room of all. I only visited other places which I liked better and want to stay there. But what about you? Where is your home?"

"Well, I've traveled around and seen other places. Now I stay in Amsterdam but I'm not home. It's just the place I live. I've always thought that you know when you are 'home.' So you could say I'm running away from home. Even now, when I'll be back in Amsterdam, I don't know what will wait for me there."

"What are you running from?"

"I don't know, it seems fun."

"Are you tired?" she said in all seriousness.

"Not yet."

"Is Hong Kong part of your home?"

"Hard to tell. This is my first time in a place completely different from what I've been used to. But strangely I feel at ease in this place. Serene, almost. I don't know the language at all, people look and behave differently, and many other things. Everything here is like a recipe for being lonely and even depressed, but for me, it feels like home just because it's foreign."

In the middle of all these people who were faceless and nameless, two people were talking about home. Fei-yan smiled at me – her first smile only for me – and said we should go home because her feet were tired. We hopped on the last train back to campus and said our goodbyes and thanks in the elevator. Back in my room I wrote in my diary that I'm starting to like the relationship I'm developing with Fei-yan even though we won't end up having sex. My satisfaction was elsewhere. I put my pen down and changed my clothes. They carried a small hint of Fei-yan's perfume, maybe from the elevator. Hollowness didn't like that. It would be best if I took a shower before going to bed. After I came back, smelling of deodorant, Hollowness lifted the blanket so I could get in. I fell asleep almost immediately and all the thoughts of Fei-yan, ghosts, cities, and talks were erased. There was nothing but Hollowness's mouldy touch and its coarse breathing. It was the only one who decided what I was allowed to dream and what not.

"Carina," she forced a smile and turned away from him.

"I saw you from across the club," Jan said pushing her hair aside. "You seem lonely. Do you need company?"

He touched her again.

"No, I'm good. Thanks."

"But I need your telephone number..."

Jan yelled it in Carina's ear and he seemed sad. Maybe because of how bad his pick-up line was, maybe because of his silly face, maybe because of the drink, maybe because he dared approach her, maybe because she hadn't got any attention for so long, or maybe because of all these things at once, Carina smiled.

"You see," he continued, "I bet my friend over there I can get your number tonight. So can you help me out?"

Carina was upset. She yelled as loud as she could, "So that's what I am to you? A bet? You'd better leave!"

Carina walked to the other side of the club, trying to find her friends.

"But don't get me wrong," Jan said after finding her ten minutes later. "I used that to be more confident."

"Just get out of here!" Carina yelled again.

The heat and the sweat became unbearable after a while, but the party didn't seem to die down. Carina was uncomfortable. Carina was dirty. Her friends found her again and downed two more Jägerbombs. She couldn't take it anymore. Carina went outside, regretting her decision to go out when she could be at home doing something productive. She stayed for a while and her skin and ears and eyes rested. The cool air woke Carina up. She wanted to go home one way or another. That was the plan. She was going to go around the club, say good night to her friends (who dumped her, but they were friends after all), and bike back to her room. Before she did all that, Jan came out of the club.

"Do you smoke?" he asked.

"I thought I told you to get lost!"

"One more chance, come on. It's just that beauty can be gut-wrenching sometimes. I saw that in a movie."

He pulled a Parliament out of his pack and handed it to

Carina. Carina struggled not to throw up.

"I don't smoke. I haven't smoked in almost a year now."

"We could share one."

Carina stood in front of the nightclub waiting for Jan to finish his cigarette. He handed it to Carina, who took a deep drag. She coughed right away. She couldn't breathe.

"Do you have that tingling sensation in your chest?"

"Yes. I don't like it."

But Carina was free now. Nobody could stop her. Maybe because of the drinks or maybe because she wanted to put her freedom to good use, she grabbed Jan's hand.

"Wait. Where's your bike?"

"There. Why?"

"Take it and follow me."

Carina biked back to her place with Jan behind her. At times, she was pedalling fast, as if she was trying to get away from something. But Jan followed. They chained their bikes outside. Carina opened the doors to the building with her magnetic key and stepped in. She took Jan by surprise and started kissing him. He smelled unexpectedly nice and his breath, although smelling like alcohol, wasn't so much of a problem.

As they walked into the elevator, Jan started kissing Carina on the neck. She pressed the button to her floor. Looking at herself in the mirror with Jan covering her and caressing her hair and biting her neck, time stopped and Carina felt guilty. She didn't even know the guy! Carina wanted Jan to stop but couldn't find the words or strength to do it. The elevator climbed slowly. She couldn't wait to get out.

Carina walked Jan by the hand towards her place. When she opened the door she was happy because she had remembered to take out the trash. She tried to turn on the light, but Jan quickly switched it back off, saying "Things are much more interesting that way." Solitude's eyes were glowing in the dark. It was at its usual spot in the corner of the room, watching, waiting for her to come back. Carina didn't like to do it in darkness; it made her sleepy. The bed was unmade and the room messy so she was relieved that Jan couldn't see how disorganized she had become. But still, at the back of her mind, Carina was empty. She couldn't relate to this man, and even though she was kissing him with the passion of a desperate lover, she didn't feel anything. She only wanted to put on her pajamas and read something. Biking all the way back to her place had sobered her up. Jan was turned on. Carina could feel the heat between his legs rubbing down her abdomen as they crashed onto the bed. In the corner, Solitude rubbed its bony hands together like the concierge of an expensive hotel welcoming a valued guest.

Carina didn't like Jan's intrusiveness. She started avoiding his kisses, and her neck and cheeks were dotted with thin layers of saliva. The places Jan visited with his lips made Carina itchy. Jan was going fast, unbuttoning his shirt, and now Carina's. His lips were kissing their way lower on Carina's neck, with a particular focus on the mole right between her breasts. Carina didn't do anything but lie on her back, arms extended on the bed. Jan almost undressed her upper half. On her ceiling, the drawers and the city lights downstairs made up strange rectangular patterns. She remembered being fascinated by the way lights come and go depending on the cars that run along the road late in the night. She barely paid any attention to Jan's kissing noises. Carina's breasts were cold.

"I can't do this."

"What?"

"I can't do this, please stop."

"What do you mean stop? We're not stopping!"

He tried to kiss her some more but Carina pushed Jan away and covered herself up.

"Listen, if you are turned on, you can use the bathroom. Just be sure not to make any mess."

Jan couldn't believe it.

"You made me come all this way for nothing!"

"Not tonight. Maybe some other time. Look, it's complicated. Best I can do is the toilet. Take it or leave it."

Jan mumbled something in Dutch – something not nice for sure – and buttoned his shirt up.

"Did you actually think it was going to be so easy? So you can just do me and then tell your friends over beer what a *lekker* night you had? I have too much freedom and I'm trying to use it the best I can. I'm making my first decisions as a free woman, but I can't be that free all of the sudden."

"I'm very happy for you. And for your freedom. But I

didn't fuck tonight and it's your fault."

"You were stupid enough to follow me."

Jan didn't say anything but Carina could read the anger on his face. Even though Solitude didn't see anything going on tonight, it was still pleased to watch the whole talk.

"You're lucky my *oma* taught me to be nice to girls."

"With those pick-up lines you used at the club? She taught you well."

"I'm going to leave."

Jan stumbled for the exit and slammed the door behind him. Carina liked his fragrance – something by Paco Rabanne. Not her favourite one, though, but still – it covered my smell. Things went smoother than she expected, so to celebrate, Carina changed her clothes, took all her makeup off before bed, and she fell asleep looking at the strange patterns on her ceiling that you could only see during the night, embracing Solitude.

As I stood in my corner, I could see Carina's kitchen on the right, the door to the bathroom on the left. The sink, the hotplates, the dishes, and the cutlery were meticulously arranged like the trophies of serial killers. I could barely hear the rumble of the refrigerator, hidden under the kitchen top, with the microwave above it, it too kept in a pristine condition. Remember me? I'm Solitude, the eagle circling around.

The central piece (and by far the most colourful) of Carina's room was the library. Its shelves were packed with books rising towards the ceiling. That was the burden Carina had to carry. She hated those books because most of them were not even hers. A collection of Eliot's poems was sitting next to Adam Smith's *An Inquiry into the Nature and Causes of the Wealth of Nations*, Kafka and Kerouac next to a book on game theory, Borges shared a shelf with something on combinatorics, but I soon got bored of describing her library. A wall of books all the way up to the ceiling, books that belong to different shelves. They were tightly pressed together in Carina's memory, otherwise one would drop here and there – but since they were so crammed together, the whole mass crumbled bit by bit anyhow.

A studio apartment in the eastern part of Amsterdam. You could either bike here on the tangled side-streets or change a couple of trams and buses, or you could take the train – from there it was only a ten-minute walk. Even though the building didn't look like much, her room was clean. In front of the library there is a bed, which, in times of need, could be converted to a double one. The bed was covered with a purple duvet that looked fluffy and warm. The floor, concrete slabs with pipes inside and a horrible vinyl top, welcomed a small green rug that stored incredible amounts of dust. Between the library and the bed there was hardly any place to cross, and yet there was a small coffee table hosting an ashtray. Next to the library, in the corner, there was a leather armchair coupled with a black reading lamp, and somewhere towards the window, a table that could be turned into a desk. The walls were decorated with butterfly stickers and some paintings I couldn't name.

The room was empty, but I could hear her coming. The gray metal door on her hallway, opening with a loud click, then closing in the same manner, her steps, rhythmically pressing against the hallway with the precision of a drummer, the key forced inside, the clicking of the lock, the knob turning. I knew exactly who it was, but the old stalking, the old hunger never ended.

Her jacket carried the smell of rain outside. She was happy she made it to her room and the warmth inside condensed the water on her glasses. She took them off. She shook the jacket she was wearing and wrapped the scarf around her back and neck. She had a knitted red shirt, a pair of jeans and some short leather boots. Her face wasn't pretty, but fascinating. Her eyes, wide and brown, seemed to belong to an intelligent person, and if we were to take her eyebrows into account, they looked authoritative, severe, even. Luckily her black eyeliner softened them up. Her cheeks were red because of the cold but most of the time she was very pale. She always used a foundation that was one or two shades lighter than her regular skin tone and she always missed a spot somewhere around her jaw-line trying to sweeten a face that was rigid. Her mouth with the end point of her lips pointing downwards would look much prettier without the shade of a mustache. Her neck, pointing outwards, and her shoulders always leaned forward, gave the impression she was always trying to reach for something she'd dropped. She took the shirt off, exposing a pair of breasts that were small but at the same time perfect for cupping with your hands. She still kept something of her adolescence even though she was considered a young woman now – at least her parents would be definitely looking for a husband if she lived in China. The beginning of a double-chin and a small layer of fat around her hips were the only things that threatened the beauty of her body. Her necklace – a fine silver chain with a semi-precious purple stone – was now behind her but that way it was easier to take it off. She rested for a moment on her bed, then from the drawer underneath, she pulled a blue towel. She then went into the bathroom and turned on the tap. She then let out a noise, indicating how cold the water came down the shower. I bet she had the goose bumps and her nipples were pointed like they were saying, *"En garde!"*

I was still waiting in my corner. The water was turned off some time ago, but she was still not getting out. From time to time you heard an electric shaver and bottles of various substances clinking on the shelf. The last thing she did before exiting was brush her teeth.

She was not done yet, and he was supposed to be here any minute. She was a bit scared, I could see that in her eyes. She was supposed to be happy, but each time she saw him she'd get something like a psychic repulsion. The line of her lips pointed even lower.

While she was getting dressed, the camera moved outside, chasing a young man who seemed to bike for his life. The rain and the wind probably helped, too. The red hands holding the handlebars, the nose trying not to let go of gushes of snot down his clothes, he was pedalling for Carina's place. His face, clean shaved, and his hair combed backwards, made him look much younger than he actually was. You might confuse him either with a Dutch hipster or a young man who had no idea what to do with his life. But in reality he was wondering what he saw in that girl he had hit on in the club a couple of weeks ago, for him to go on several dates with her, after she had had the guts to say no to him? His father always taught him that in life he should pursue two kinds of girls only: the quiet ones, and the ones that were hard to get (they're usually worth it). His only hope was that they would stop taking advantage of each other after some time and perhaps stop talking or get serious about it. He couldn't bear leaving her knowing that she would suffer. Surprising even for him.

He rang the intercom and the person from upstairs buzzed him in. He took the stairs and knocked on the gray metal door. He waited in front of the door with a sense of impatience and agitation, waiting to see her figure, but when the door opened he could not say a word. His eyes seemed to fail him, he didn't feel more alive or even dead. There was nothing but silence in his head.

"Hello Carina."

"Hello Jan."

Carina helped him take off his wet coat and handed him a towel for his head. In his light blue buttoned shirt, Jan sat on the bed, wiping himself. The purple duvet did not go well at all with his shirt and it looked like Jan was an alien element on top of the bed. He was nervous because no other woman groomed herself so much for him. He wondered if that was the thing that kept him going. Carina sat next to Jan on the purple duvet. He stroked her hair and asked if she was sad. She wasn't, but maybe the line of her lips pointing downwards made him ask. In any case, when he read the book, *How to Date Girls*, a good tip was to ask about the other person's feelings. Some gestures of tenderness would always be welcome. This dating thing wasn't so bad. Check check check.

Her voice was higher pitched than usual, like one of those young but incredibly annoying secretaries who can't buzz people in to the boss. But Jan knew where this was going. The discussion was going to follow some conventional topics and things were going to get cozier and cozier. Only after that they'd get to the interesting stuff. Carina told him she doesn't like the rain outside.

Suddenly, she stood up and said she was going to make some coffee. She reminded Jan he wasn't allowed to stay on her bed with his wet pair of black jeans (at least for now) and invited him to sit on the armchair. As she stood up, she smelled Jan's hair and couldn't understand how someone's hair could smell like grilled beef no matter how many times it got washed. Carina always gave Jan the same towel and when she went to the bathroom to hang it to dry, she would sniff it. It was contaminated, and it was possibly a lost cause trying to clean it, but she was okay with that. When Carina walked out of the bathroom, much to the delight of Jan who secretly liked seeing her legs walking Carina back and forth through the room, she asked how was Jan's day at the Burger Bar. Then Jan would make the same joke about him flipping burgers, the same joke Carina didn't laugh at even when she heard it the first time, the same uncomfortable silence settling in following Jan's diminishing laughter.

Carina put the coffee in the coffee machine, and as she was squeezing it out, Jan stood up and placed his hand over Carina's. He then grabbed her from the waist trying to speed up the night. He knew they were still at the beginning, and he knew things should be taken somewhat gradually (that's what it said in *How to Date Girls*) otherwise it would look abusive and disgusting. Jan lost his patience for a brief moment. He was inexperienced with how this whole dating thing went, that was all. Jan wanted to drop the conversation and squeeze Carina in his arms, but then all that good coffee would go to waste and Carina was a very efficient person.

Over coffee, they talked about the most trivial things. Carina told him about the books she was reading at the moment, important economic theories, using lots of numbers, dates, and other math-related things. Jan told her about the best places to get burgers in Amsterdam, and that wasn't the Burger Bar. There were other places, somewhere close to the market next to the Heineken brewery, and they should go there sometime even though he worked at a different place. Look, he could even draw a map on a piece of paper, "Do you have some so I can show it to you?" Carina's silence and condescending smile made him rethink the things he was saying. *"Stupid, talk about things you're both interested in. CHAPTER III!"* But Jan was so impatient! He only said these things so that time could go by faster. But she didn't show any signs of giving up.

Women could delay the things you wanted for so long they could have driven you insane. Carina had the habit of telling her day in the most minute detail, talking to Jan about friends and people he will most likely never meet: "She did this, he did this, I did that, the time was 15:00. Oh, and he hooked up with this other girl she didn't like," and many, many more things. Jan tuned out and started focusing on caressing Carina. At times she would pause for a moment or two, then go on with her day, then back and forth until she gave up. If he hadn't been used to it, Jan would believe Carina was stalling. They lie down.

After a while.

Covered by the purple duvet and with caffeine running around, Jan stroked Carina's skin. Every time after they did it, after Jan stared into Carina's enormous pupils, almost being swallowed by them and just when he was about to come, he saw an explosion of colour in her eyes, just like that time when he went to Ibiza and dropped acid with his friends. Fractals, geometric shapes that turn into familiar faces and then melt into one another, cold colours, warm colours, cold-warm colours, a pleasant warmth like Dutch summer sun or the heat from the giant grills at the Burger Bar, sizzling and thunderstorms. The kind of lights you would see at a club or party. And then, hearing the rhythm of the rain, everything seemed to work well in the universe. Of course, he wouldn't dare tell such things to Carina, he would look even more awkward than usual, but maybe that was the thing he was after, the thing that kept him returning and seeing Carina, that burst of colour in a girl he hit on some time ago.

Once everything was done, Jan liked the way Carina's flesh softened, as if she released the tension in her body. Her arms, her neck, her face were not saying anything anymore. They stayed like this for a minute or two and began telling stories. That's what they did until early morning, when Jan had to leave for work again. Even though it was somewhere around 8:00 by the time Jan biked back to the Burger Bar, he was in a very good mood, like a relief almost to get away from Carina's room. Jan told Carina that he was not a morning person but the moments they shared in her bed kept him going throughout much of the day. He had something to think of when flipping the burgers or fries or the grilled vegetables and bacon. Carina was also happy. After she recovered from the post-sex silence, she started the discussion by saying something like, "I have never been so wet in my life, but there is something missing." That always hurt Jan's pride, who envisioned himself being good at precisely two things: making the perfect burger and knowing how to show a girl a good time. Jan tried asking what went wrong and how could he improve, but Carina either started sobbing or gave him the silent treatment. After all there was that Dutch saying, *meten is weten*. To measure is to know. At work, Jan received intricate graphs, statistics and other points of improvement every month to know what he did right and what were the things he should focus on more, but maybe how good you were in bed couldn't be measured by numbers or other quantifiers (he learned the term from Carina). "One day," she said, "I'll tell you what you need to know, but give me some more time." And that's what Jan did. He read in chapter IV of *How to Date Girls* that he shouldn't force talk about things they weren't comfortable about if he wanted to have a serious relationship. So far, Jan did a good job.

The same thing couldn't be said about Carina. If there ever was a book on *How to Date Guys*, she definitely had to read chapter IV. Before engaging in one of her stories, Carina would always ask some of the most uncomfortable things about Jan: How many girls he slept with, did he think of himself as having a big penis, had he ever seen another guy's penis and compared himself, had he ever slept with two girls at the same time, did he and his friend have sex with the same woman, did he ever put it in a girl's ass, does he have any weird sex things (she once suggested he should lend her his Burger Bar uniform if he didn't like Carina dressing up like a school-girl) and other dirty stuff. Jan would laugh nervously and answer negatively or find clever (but that wasn't his strong point) ways of diverting her direct questions that were to the point of becoming rude. Even though Jan was struggling to give honest answers, Carina always said something like, "You're lying, there's something you're not telling me, you're hiding something." Out of the few nights they spent together at Carina's (and it was always at Carina's), these moments were the strangest for Jan. He learned after the third time how they should go about it, the dial on the intercom, the undressing, the coffee, the small talk, the sex, and the other steps, but there was something very strange about Carina's spear-like questions. Whenever the algorithm of the night naturally developed into this barrage of what some people might consider *piquant* details of a *medewerker* at the Burger Bar, Jan was uncomfortable but he never dared not to tell. Who knows what might have happened if she was denied her answers? But no matter what they were, Carina still didn't believe them, and Jan was okay with that. She wasn't interested in hearing the "right" or "wrong" answer, just "the" answer. And because of that, Jan transformed himself into such a character that he could no longer distinguish what was "true" from what was "wrong." And so, whenever Carina asked how many girls Jan had slept with, he would answer something like, "You know how it is, there is a big difference between having sex and making love. I've only made love with four or five women, and those are the ones I remember best. The rest, they are just conquests, you know, pure arrogance." Carina would mock him every chance she'd get. She was particularly happy with embarrassing him, and in time Jan got used to it, even though half of the time he couldn't get why Carina laughed at him or burst into laughter and then apologized. He was being very serious, and this chick laughed in his face. "Sorry," she said, "I picked this thing up from my ex. He was always making fun of everything I said, even when I was nice to him, that arrogant prick." And then they always came around to the "ex." Who was he, what was he all about, what happened? Every time Jan asked, more out of a sense of pride, Carina always turned it around, postponing things. "Never mind him, he's not here anymore. I'll tell the story another time." Was he dead? There were two things Carina was most elusive about: the way the night progressed and the discussion about "the ex." For Jan it didn't matter, he had his fun. No matter who this "ex" was, he had to know what his story was because Carina was obviously protecting him. And they had sex! They shared their most intimate parts and yet she wouldn't open up to Jan, she wouldn't tell who this guy was. Jan actually said that one night and Carina was so furious with him he had to dress and leave before the time was up. "So that's what I am to you? One of those chicks you bang and that's it?" "Arguably," said Jan trying to act smart again. "Just get out!" Gut-wrenching feeling ensued in the cold streets of Amsterdam. Jan was almost certain that there was nothing special about this guy, but Carina had to make such a fuss about it! "I'm pretty sure if I actually heard the story, I'd be like, 'That's it? That's what you were so sensitive about?'" On the other hand, Carina was interested in hearing everything the *medewerker* of the Burger Bar had to say about his previous relationships. Everything up to the most minute details: how they had sex, what was her favourite position, did she let you do bad things to her, did she dress up for you the way I did, was she prettier than me, was she wetter than me, did she scream the way I did, did you go out for dates, did you show her the best burger place in Amsterdam. And again it was Jan's turn to feel uncomfortable. He didn't like this game of going back and forth and just about when he was about to speak his mind, Carina would always go on into one of her stories, and she talked and talked until morning.

Carina ran her hand through Jan's hair and then sniffed her fingers, aroused by the smell of grilled beef. There was something primitive about this, about Jan, that she hadn't found previously in that ex of hers. Jan was a provider – a worker, and he took pride in his job and he was good at it. Flipping burgers and feeding people was a serious matter. And of course, it was the Burger Bar, not something crappy like McDonald's or Burger King. His job took some skill, and one day Jan dreamed of running his own Burger Bar. He was going to call it, *Jan's Burger Bar*. Jan was a real man, from the real world. His struggles were real, he lived in the present, he didn't think things while staring out of the window like some washed-up philosopher. Whenever he had something to say, he said it. When he had to get the job done, then he'd get the job done. A meat and potatoes kind of guy. Of course, he was trying to act smart just to impress her, but Carina found his attempts cute. Jan was just like the smell in his hair: raw. She liked hearing him constantly complaining about work, about how things could be run much more efficiently ("One day, when I'll have my own Burger Bar...") but how his stupid colleagues were in it just for the salary, which was a little bit better than the minimum wage. And all his ranting about how his benefits are decreasing every year, and those Romanians and Bulgarians and Moroccans coming to steal all their jobs for half the money seemed so far away from Carina. She wondered if she would have the same struggles once she was going to be done with university. And of course, there was this girl at his workplace – Jan used to go to her place for a coffee every now and then. But we all knew what was going to happen with that coffee. Later Jan would have had no problem in paying that co-worker of his a visit, but, "Nobody makes such a nice coffee like you, Carina." Jan was troubled and not paying attention to his co-worker's needs. That girl suspected Jan was seeing somebody else, but Jan always denied it. "And that makes it even more obvious!" his co-worker said while greeting the new customers with a smile on her face. "That's why I said 'arguably' back then," Jan tried to defend himself. "Because I'm having something very different with you. I don't want to be seen like I am taking advantage of you, but between you and me, you are the one who hides things. I want to know you better. You intrigue me. Do you know how hard it is to fry that bacon while thinking about you and your stories? You have to be very careful with bacon, because it can get burned very easily. If I was at my co-worker's, I wouldn't have these nice talks with you, maybe about work and burgers, and who knows, maybe this is it for me."

Maybe this was, indeed! Who knew what lay ahead of them. But Carina couldn't picture herself next to Jan or any other guy for that matter. A few economic theories, a few medium-rare burgers, a few years, a few grilled vegetables and bacon – those were the things that made people grow apart.

Carina looked for Jan's shirt. She buttoned up and went for the bathroom. The final stage of the night was almost up. Hearing the water running and perhaps some tubes being squeezed out, Jan jumped out of bed (it was alright, it was still dark) and looked for his coat. He pulled out his pack of tobacco, some papers, and filters, and he rolled a cigarette. He opened the window and nearly bumped into me. Have to be more careful with him, I couldn't reveal myself just yet. Jan smoked his cigarette by the window, naked. The sound of rain pounding on the metal window-sill made his hair stand up. The buildings around Carina's studio, the *tabaksmagazijn* downstairs, the small bridge where ducks were sleeping meant nothing to him. Outside Carina's window, everything ended. There was nobody, not even the night buses or some late bikers down the street, nothing. Civilization ended. *This* was the place he was supposed to be, *this* was the only place that held any meaning for Jan. Throwing his cigarette down out of the window and closing it, Jan got under the purple duvet, shivering. Just in time. Carina got out of the bathroom and sniffed. She would usually argue strongly against anyone smoking in her room, but with Jan it was a different story. His hair and the cigarettes turned her on even more. The things combined made her think of some fat, greasy guy flipping burgers for a family barbecue. She sniffed once more before getting back in bed and gently scolding Jan for bringing the cold in bed. They kissed and caressed each other for a short while.

After that, Carina said all of a sudden, "Do you want to know his story?"

W hen my mom caught me smoking my first cigarette at sixteen, her main problem was what I was going to do when I was twenty. She tore up my newly bought red Marlboro's and threw the packet in the rubbish bin. Drug addict? Alcoholic? Something along those lines.

Now I'm a bit over twenty and luckily I'm not a drug addict. I drink and smoke but that's pretty much it. I don't know why exactly I do it or how "cool" it is. I don't like the hangovers the day after, and each time I tell myself I should be drinking more water. Alcohol weakens the bonds between your neurons and even if it's liquid, it dehydrates you. Like coffee. Some people drink to forget, others to remember, others because they want to start a fight or do something stupid, and others just to let off some steam. I need these from time to time.

We did it on a Friday night. Wan Chai, a place in the centre of Hong Kong, was an ordinary area by day and decadent by night. As you leave the train at exit C and come out at Lockhart Road, there is a wide boulevard with bars and nightclubs on each side. Taxis patrol the streets picking up all sorts of drunk people. Wealthy Englishmen in suits and ties, young people, prostitutes, Asians, blacks, Indians, nationless, colourless, assign themselves to a pub or club and just drink until they throw up and then drink some more. I couldn't get why the people (including me) dressed up so nicely when all they did was to show what animals they were. I loved the place. The stench of stale beer and the gas of the cars, combined with the sweaty armpits of the Englishmen and the cheap perfume of the streetwalkers would make any god from any religion rain fire and stone upon them.

Because we were students, we looked for the places that were the most cost-efficient. There is a bar with ten Hong Kong dollar tequila shots? Let's go! What's that? Four giant beers for a hundred Hong Kong dollars? Sure, why not! Free entry to a club if you're a student? Gotta go, gotta go! Vodka and Red Bull for just a hundred and fifty? Are you kidding me? Want to share a pack of Luckies? Pleasure doing business! The centre of Lockhart Road, however, was the 7-Eleven. The drinks were cheap and the lines were so long that it reminded me of the stories my mom used to tell me about her times and the lines for bread and milk.

For some reason I didn't have dinner that night so I got drunk pretty fast. The air was so charged up with alcohol you could get tipsy by just standing there, and inhaling a couple of times. Walking into the bars you would feel like stepping into different worlds: Irish pubs, English bars, live music bars, nightclubs of all kinds and themes, exotic women offering their bodies for a modest fee, people puking and pissing in the side-streets, soft drugs, hard drugs sold by suspicious people at the corners of the streets.

I also lost my group pretty fast. The city ate them up. But then I remembered Fei-yan was supposed to join in as well with her friend. Earlier in the day she told me she was going to have dinner with a faceless and nameless person. She said she missed the taste of German beer and the sausages and the *rollbraten*. So I called and met her shortly after at the train exit.

"So this must be the guy you told me everything about!" her friend who tagged along said.

"Hi there, I'm..."

"No need for your name! Fei-yan told me so much about you!"

"Really?"

"Of course! Girls talk about a lot of things, you know? I'm Catherine."

"I'm happy to meet you."

"Same here."

Fei-yan called some people to find out where they were. I said nothing to Fei-yan and continued to chat up her friend. If you weren't paying enough attention, you could say we were full-on flirting. Fei-yan was quiet as we walked around all those drunk people but I saw her taking sneak peeks at us. It made me smile. Catherine was overly excited to have finally met me. I knew nothing about this girl, and yet she talked to me as if we'd known each other since the Big Bang. To spice things up and also because I was drunk, it seemed a good idea at that time to see if Fei-yan liked me or not. Funny how high-school never seems to end. So then I told Catherine, "Oh, it's so nice that Fei-yan decided to bring you along!" or "I didn't know Fei-yan had such nice friends," or "I liked you before, but now I'm liking you even more!" And just so she could barely hear it, "Perhaps even more than Fei-yan!" Catherine giggled at everything I said and it was annoying. I was itching to say something nasty, something that could put off that crazy excitement of hers but then I would have missed the big picture here. So I swallowed my bad thoughts with a big bottle of Japanese beer and hoped to see some results. Fei-yan was smiling at us, even remarking how nicely we seemed to be getting along with each other, but her insides were boiling. It doesn't matter how good you are or where you come from, jealousy is something you cannot hide.

We met the rest of our group at a live music bar. The band was playing some classic straight rock from the 1970s and 1980s, perfect for the 40-year-olds dancing to the covers and making fools of themselves. As soon as I got there, one of my friends handed me a huge glass of beer and I had to compete with him in a chugging contest. Loudly encouraged by the crowd and accompanied by announcements from the band, I lost. I was never able to chug beer as fast as other people. Still, a free beer is a free beer. Fei-yan and Catherine both got a mojito.

The band went on playing these old songs and it sounded pretty good. The atmosphere inside was starting to resemble the one outside. A Japanese woman in her late 30s started dancing with me and dragged me to her table. I had no idea where Fei-yan was. I could not see the Japanese woman well, but she was stroking my hands and fingers as we were sitting at the table. Was that a ring on her finger? I asked her where she was from, and then she said something about Tokyo or Osaka. I told her I knew this writer, Murakami and that he was good. For some reason she got very excited about this and called her friend. They talked in Japanese and I only understood "Murakami" and then they both smiled at me. Still caressing my palms and fingers, she made her hand into a fist and took it close to her mouth while her head made a back and forth motion. "Bathroom, okay?" But the bathroom was full so I was disappointed. After all, a kiss and a blowjob were the same, right? I thought she had a piercing in her tongue, but then it somehow ended up in my mouth when we started kissing but she said "Take, take, is okay!" She then gave me her drink to swallow it down. Where was everybody? Looking around the bar, almost all the people were gone. I didn't notice when the band stopped playing. I watched the Japanese woman going to one of the members and kissing him on the mouth. He was wearing a ring also. I wanted to go to that man and warn him not to get kissed again. Who knows, maybe I wasn't the only one who tried to get a free blowjob in the bathroom of the bar where the guy was playing.

I had to take a piss. The cleaners had already started to do their thing so nothing worked to make them let me in. The law was the law. So then I took it to a side-street. Trash, huge cockroaches, and half-digested food. Pissing, I tried to aim for one of these bugs, who, I swear to God, were as big as my palm. On the opposite side of the dimly lit alley, an Indian-looking guy with a British accent was pissing too. I started laughing because there was nobody else apart from him, me, and the bugs. Just like you would have blood brothers, we were the piss brothers of a side street in Wan Chai. All of the sudden he found his face in a cracked mirror and with his pants halfway down he started shouting: "Look at you, man! Look at you! Look how far you've come in life! You're young, handsome, you got the dream job, you have a girlfriend and a place to stay! You deserve that shit man! You're hardworking!" I felt like laughing at my piss brother as a sign of appreciation, but I could only look into the eyes of a 7-Eleven saleswoman and then back to the huge hairy mole on her cheek as she jumped over my stream of piss trying to get to the back door of the shop. That look took away a part of my innocence.

I was forgetting myself, I was turning myself into art. Art that forgets itself is the highest degree of abandonment possible for a human being.

I don't know when it hit me, but when it did, it did. Walking on the main road I somehow managed to land in front of a nightclub. The bouncer ushered me in. A new set of songs was getting ready, so people were just standing or going outside for a smoke or drink. Slowly, a drumbeat crept into the audio system of the club and a wave-like sound bounced between the left and right side of the dance floor. This wasn't just a nightclub song. The DJ turned up the volume slowly and placed the sound of a metronome on top of all that. I couldn't distinguish among the faceless and nameless people who poured back in. Things were moving so fast around me that they looked like an endless stream of red, green and yellow strips, just like you would watch a high-speed train whizzing by; but everything I did happened very slowly, like those dreams you have when trying to escape from someone but can't. The DJ raised the number of pulses on the metronome so that it soon became an endless stream of sharp tones and my ears couldn't take it anymore. The lights went out and I could see the people for a fraction of a second like an x-ray machine would. Skulls, rib cages, femurs, all of it in one blink of the strobe. As the song dropped, concentric circles and hearts made of dirty gold shot beams of light to other circles and hearts around the walls of the club at 90-degree angles to the beat of the drums and then I could see Carina and Fei-yan dancing next to me, rubbing themselves against me, pulling my shirt, shoving their hands in my hair, biting my neck, leaving lipstick traces on my collar, touching my belt with their fingers and they were there, I swear it, their perfume was like no other. Carina and Fei-yan were in white and red. The lights changed every eight bars so that you would have one red and the other white. Just like the others, I couldn't tell who was which but at that point it didn't matter. Another layer was added to the song and the bass line was making its way to the front. A rain of numbers and green binary codes fell onto the dance floor as the DJ input the sounds in his set and the floor turned and the lights changed to a series of fast moving satellite images that showed places from all around the world, places I've been to and places I will never know. Fei-yan and Carina's movements left traces like the algae I saw in my hike so I was not just dancing with them, I was seeing maybe five Carinas and five Fei-yans at the same time. Red-white, white-red, the girls were touching the people around them and each time they did they turned into beams of light and the sound they made while becoming both waves and radiation accompanied some nice insertions and harmonies in the beat of the song. The people were made of music. I could hear my heart beat and my breathing. Then I said it would be really cool if they could make out with each other. Both of them smiling at me, they went at it with such ferocity that it made my insides feel funny. Kissing each other, caressing their bodies in a way that wasn't vulgar, they became a beam of light and the centre of the club. Fei-yancarina or CarinaFei-yan, redwhite or whitered exploded into music, approaching a climax that resembled the music of angels and I witnessed that moment. The people were drawn to them like insects to fire and they all melted down into the same music that once created the universe only to be sucked in by it and cancel each other. The flash was so bright that for a second I thought I was going to be carried away myself but instead, I just figured out where I was. There were two girls making out in front of me but they weren't who I thought they were. I got out of the club and ran into my friends, who were looking for me. They needed one more guy to share a cab. Fei-yan was with them and looked tired. She rested her head on my bony shoulder for the entire trip back to the campus. She hadn't been in that nightclub at all. ******

I was supposed to meet Fei-yan on the stairs of her floor. The plan was to go back to our dorms after our cab ride and continue drinking there. I really wanted to sleep, so I said I was going to pass. In my room, getting ready to snuggle with Hollowness, Fei-yan texted me saying "Meet me on the stairs. My floor ten mins." Hollowness saw me smiling as I received the text and turned the other way in bed. It was late, and because of the cameras, I couldn't take the elevator to Fei-yan's place. I was still drunk and predicting one of those hangovers that will make you lose your will to live for three days. But the taxi back and running up the stairs woke me a bit. I changed my clothes and went up. Fei-yan was waiting for me. The hallway was narrow. Out of the window, the sun was beginning to rise. She wore only a long white shirt and some flip-flops. "These are my PJs." She had painted her toenails a bright red. We smiled at each other and I tried to act sober.

"I should not have brought Catherine with me."

"Why?"

"Because she said she liked you."

"Is that so? Can I have her number?"

"Not a chance."

"But I barely talked to her. How can you like someone so fast? Or am I that good?"

"Just shut up."

"You are so into me."

Then I started laughing, the laughter of a person who knew he had somebody else's heart in his hands.

"You are so into me."

"Shut up! Someone might hear you!" Fei-yan said in all

seriousness.

"I knew it."

"I did not say anything."

"You don't need to. You were jealous. I can figure it out."

"Self-illusion is very dangerous, Ulysses."

"I like you too."

"Of course. Everyone does. The ones I like back matter."

"Right."

Fei-yan was struggling not to cry. She tried looking at me a couple of times but she bit her lip, forcing her not to do it. She could only gather the strength to say:

"You are leaving."

The way she bit her lip turned me on. The way she was struggling not to cry was even hotter. I came closer to her on the steps. I was leaving and something inside my chest melted.

"Don't cry."

"I am not crying for you!" she replied angrily.

What was I to do? I couldn't think straight for so many reasons and everything I would say would be inappropriate.

"Life is unfair, huh?"

"Cut it out."

"Do you think we'll see each other again?"

"I would very much like to. Yes."

"Did you read *Don Quixote*?"

"Of course, who hasn't?"

"I don't know, it's just that everyone seems to know him but hasn't read the actual book. You know, that old man who thought he was a knight-errant and travels around and has all these adventures?"

"Yes, I know him!" Fei-yan said exasperatedly.

"Right. What do you like most about him?"

"I do not know. It is a sad story."

"Do you want to know my favourite scene from *Don Quixote*?"

"Yes?"

"There is a part where Don Quixote needs to get down into this well and fight a demon because the villagers believed it was cursed. But as the people lower him down, Don Quixote falls asleep. And he has this fantastic dream where he fights all these dragons and devils and all sorts of creatures. And when the people pull him back up, he said he defeated everything and the well was safe again."

"You are too drunk for this to work."

"Maybe I'm not that good at telling a story, or maybe I'm one of those drunks that gets lucid the more he drinks, but that's how I feel about this place. Not so much the demons, but the dream part. Hong Kong isn't probably the best city in the world and there are many wrong things about this place, but the things I've seen, the people I've met, the people I've come to like, it's all just a big dream for me. And it sucks, because most of these people I'll never see again."

"What do you mean?"

"You."

"You do not want to see me again?"

"I want to. But I might not."

"Why do you like Don Quixote?" she said after a while.

"Because of his faith. Of course, he gives it up in the end and Sancho struggles with what to do next because Don Quixote's faith is contagious. I think that everyone is a great-great-great-cousin or uncle or aunt or grandson of Don Quixote. His story is our story. It's a story about faith. Numbers, religion, facts, it's all faith. Don Quixote really believed those windmills were giants. And that's how I feel about you now. I'm not saying you're a giant or something, it's just that I have this faith I will see you again and things are going to be great when it's going to happen. I know this can go wrong in so many ways, but if we don't lose each other, then we will meet sooner than you'd think. I wasn't looking for anything, really, I was running, but then you came along. My dad always told me that the things you lose come back to you the moment you stop looking for them and he was right. I found you and you found me. And here we are, sitting on these cold steps on your floor, and I'm still drunk but I'm trying not to show it. I even brushed my teeth before coming here, because I am secretly hoping to kiss you tonight, can you smell it? Somewhere down there, you're a relative of Don Quixote yourself, don't you think? Why were you jealous in the first place, why me out of all your pool of suitors? You don't know me very well, you don't know where I come from or where I've been and I'm leaving soon. For you, I'm just a terminally-diseased patient, but that's what makes it hot in the first place, right? Isn't that a fancy way of saying faith? I'm going to write letters to you, maybe I'm going to leave one in your mailbox when you come back from the airport after you send me off, and once you read it you'll feel even worse because I'm not there anymore. And I'm going to keep writing letters to you because who writes letters these days? It's a lost art, really. And I'll write because I will miss you and I'll even try to cry on the plane and I never cry and I'm going to say it to you once and never admit it again. I'll write you a couple more letters from Amsterdam, maybe three or four at the most and say I don't want to taint your touch with another woman's, because I am one of the few real gentlemen left on this planet but how long is this going to last? And I'll think about the times we spent together, the meals we shared, the tea in your room that changed something, your stories; and I'll dream about you every once in a while. And in my letters I'll write 'Fei-yan, I've loved you like a man loves a woman he never touches, only writes to, keeps little photographs of,' and that's the way Bukowski said it. You're going to be my celluloid lover and in my head I'll always picture the moment when we'll meet again and repeat it in my head time and again just like the Buddhist monks because I am Don Quixote's great-great-great-great-grandson. And I can imagine you and your little quirks, I'll imagine you being touched by other lovers and be incredibly jealous but it's all in my head. And hearing you cry about your failed love stories like this one so I can write to you, 'Fei-yan, all lovers betray,' and feel better about myself. And you know, once I stop the letters, once we no longer skype every day, once our sleeping pattern gets adjusted to not staying awake until morning and chatting online, once we grow apart from each other, because you know, people grow apart all the time, next year, or after five years, heck, after fifteen years, when you see me again, once you get married and have kids and see me for the second time, now that's going to be a sad end for it because then I'll lose faith, like Don Quixote did. If I meet you in a different place at a different time, I'll probably be unfair to you and you'll be unfair to me. And then I'll look at you and then all of it will come back to me because I've forgotten you or because I kept your memory somewhere in my head or in my notebooks and hid you in a dusty drawer, and then I'll say, 'Yes, you and I, we shared something a while ago.' It's *almost* a love story. And I really can't blame you. You know, I'm just going on a rant here."

Fei-yan stood there listening, struggling not to cry and smiling. Something inside her melted.

"So you do not believe a single word of what you just said, you shallow man?"

"I once met a girl who said she liked me very much and she was drunk. When I asked her the next day, she said I shouldn't believe a drunk girl."

"So that was it? You were hitting on me with nice letters and all?"

"You also have that Latin saying, do you know it? *In vino veritas*. In wine lies the truth. So you could say I was telling the truth because I was drunk. I never say these incredibly nice things for free, that's for sure. If only Carina knew..."

"Who?"

"This girl, Carina. It's not important."

"Tell me."

"Don't worry, there will be time. Gimmie a break here! I've been pouring my heart out in front of you and you're asking me about this other girl?"

"I am curious about you."

"Any comments, questions, suggestions on what I just said?"

"What do you want me to say? It was very nice. I just finished reading *Siddartha* by Herman Hesse, do you know it? In this book there is a passage that says, 'Worthy of love and admiration were these people in their blind loyalty, their blind strength and tenacity.' I liked it very much. Having faith in something makes you worthy of love and admiration."

"You're just hiding yourself behind this book. Are you saying I'm worthy of love and admiration?"

"Maybe."

"It's very hard for you to say these things, isn't it?"

"It is. I do not know how to say them and I do not want to ruin all the nice things you said so far, even though you are drunk now and you do not make much sense. It also made me think about the people who are in long-distance relationships. They are ascetics. Have you ever had a long-distance relationship? Maybe with Carina?"

"I know it's very fashionable these days to have such a thing, but I didn't have one. And I don't plan on having one either."

"Really?"

"Yes. I know you tried to talk about us right now, but I can never ask this from you, Fei-yan. It's just not fair for either of us. Do you believe in destiny? Do you believe that somewhere in this sky, well, you can't see them right now since we are sitting on some stairs, but do you believe that some stars were aligned in such a way that people's lives are set right from their birth?"

"I do not know."

"You want to know what I think? This girl, Carina, said people never change and I didn't believe that. Something changed. I don't know when, but it did and I know all these things I'm saying right now might be too much and too all of the sudden. But with you, I met you by chance, and here I am a couple of months later saying a bunch of nice things. What about destiny? A last-minute phone call, sleeping in, I don't know, there are a million other things that could've gone wrong and we wouldn't be having this conversation right here. I would just have passed you on the street and been okay with it. And who knows how many more moments both of us missed just because of another thing happening in between? And if there is such a thing called destiny, if there is a star that controls the fate of men and women, then I will meet you again, just like I met you the first time."

Fei-yan went silent. There wasn't so much left to be said anyway.

"Faith is also a way of fooling yourself. Just like in Don Quixote."

"I know. Sun's almost up."

I dragged myself closer to Fei-yan. My jeans were touching her leg. I was nervous and my hands were sweaty and shaking. I could have touched her back and found out she was not wearing a bra under the shirt but I didn't want to leave a sweaty stain. I crossed my hand through her hair in a way that made everything look incredibly creepy. She was looking down to her red-painted toenails and my smile made it uncanny. The birds outside were singing, "twit twit twit!"

"Fei-yan?"

"Yes?" she said turning her head towards me seeming surprised at how close our faces were.

"I'm going for it."

I started leaning in.

"No."

"Really?" I was still leaning in.

"NO."

She looked down again and shook her back. She wanted my hand out of there. I moved away to the other end of the steps. What was I going to say? So rudely forced.

"I think we should go to bed."

"Good idea."

"We are both very tired."

"Yes we are."

"Lunch tomorrow?"

"Sure. Sleep tight."

"You too."

I climbed the steps down to my floor. I could taste the bitterness of rejection with a hint of toothpaste on the back of my tongue. Hollowness was not yet asleep but this time I didn't hold it in my arms, and the way we were sleeping in the opposite directions of the bed, we formed the perfect symmetry of a butterfly's wings.

Not knowing what to say, Jan stood in silence. When Carina didn't say anything, he only mumbled a short "Yes."

"It's time for me to introduce you to him. The bathroom is probably one of the places where you make the most important decisions. I don't want to be judged and I don't want you telling me I'm hiding something. If there ever was a role for me and you in this whole story, then it's going to be over once I finish what I have to say. Because *this* is not about me and you, it's about *him* and our paths and I tried stalling for as long as I could, I've given lengthy descriptions and fillers, but how long can you put up with this? Truth is, I was only masking the end. I just needed somebody to listen. This is our last night together."

Jan was uncertain about what Carina just said to him. Like a small child before bed or before work, he was expecting a nice story about Prague or her family and friends, but the thing Carina said made the hair on his legs stand up, just like when he smoked his cigarette three minutes ago. He couldn't understand, but it had something to do with his end as a listener, as a character, as a worker at the *Burger Bar* and as a person.

All Jan's other senses died out. Even though his eyes were used to the dark and Carina's features were becoming more evident, his hearing extended through every pore of his skin, through every hair. They were all directed at Carina like a huge group of parabolic antennae. Her words were becoming substance, and he was the insect who witnessed the wonder. Forget Jan the worker at the Burger Bar, forget the perfect burger and the grilled vegetables and bacon, everything he ever did so far in his life as a character and as a person melted down into this moment even though he didn't know it.

"I am listening," he said.

"I have known this person for six years and three months, so more than a quarter of my life, two of which I spent with him in a relationship. We were classmates in high school, but he came two weeks later than the rest of us and he said there was a mistake with the computer and he was actually supposed to be here, where I was the first one to say hello to him, my you should have seen him so confused and scared there was him walking the hallways of the high school trying not to wake someone who is sleeping like his long hair very few guys had long hair back then with blue eyes he looked like your typical writer or a misunderstood painter like me romanticizing things right now but stories slip into a cheap romanticism without even realizing it that later on I thought when he was sensitive to everything that happened around anyone who knew him would tell you he was making fun of everything and everyone and he was very loud and arrogant when he wanted you to see the truth of a sad lonely guy who had no idea how to talk to people about the problems he had the first few days past you were with me not so long ago because I could see how girls are when they are fifteen or sixteen aiming at the guys in their senior year or who knows even better than a guy in my year who was not yet ready for my love in the future where people need guidance to hold on to besides a sense of purpose when they would go crazy like we did get together in the last year of high school but we weren't just friends when I had to keep a certain amount of interest for when the time comes to have my own fun receiving attention from other guys below his remembrance of some things past his fun and other girls was dating at that time of poor choices to get my attention for some reasons I don't remember stopped talking for almost a year with each other every day in school but we had our fights here and there as it came over me on his eighteenth birthday on a fourth of January I wanted to sleep with him when he did it before with somebody I hadn't and we were there on the bed almost ready and he said No Thank You for getting dressed back with the anger before remembering things passed in my life and pride as a soon to be woman ready to do it that I didn't even imagine he would say no to me nobody says no to me understand me he was pressured to be the first one to get imprinted onto a girl's mind forever when you took something you couldn't give back to you can't biologically give it back because there are surgeries where they can restore the virginity of the moment has to be special to do this but at the same time I wasn't ready for that which I had to just go and throw myself in the arms of some other guy I'd decided I'll have sex with just to get it over with the good thing in my mind and in my pants deciding that if I ever had sex with him in this life I should rob him of the honour of being the first to tell him I think I'm in love with you on the Christmas Eve of our final year of high school and a week later on January 1st we did it at my place for some reason things started getting sour around the time we came to Amsterdam maybe it's because both of us were among strangers that don't speak Dutch and we had to look out for one another when my dad told him that he should take care of me no matter what and that's something his dad used to say to him whenever he'd leave for a longer period of time with his work there he did take care of me and in that world that wasn't ours we were becoming more and more important to each other as the days went on for ages when people change when they travel Dutchmen outside the Netherlands and boy can they drink a lot and be incredibly rude like not so much here in Amsterdam where people ride their bikes and smile to one another on the streets but outside this small city they become free and show their nature of having something to do with how Amsterdam works for the foreigners in the same way you complained about it a lot when you said tourists come to Amsterdam just to get high and fuck some prostitutes from Eastern Europe or whatever poor place they come from and you miss so much if you do only that's what Amsterdam is famous for being the Sodom and Gomorrah of Europe unionizing this isn't true because I've lived here for so long and I understood your point of view frustrating when I saw all those people in the centre of the city getting high out of their minds just because it's legal to get high I'm sure you can do it everywhere but still Amsterdam keeps this image of a place where everything is permitted even though it's not true to the Dutchmen who behave the way they do outside their home city because the fines are not as big as they are in Amsterdam I guess you guys are just more direct than other people are and I'm fine with that freedom around us we couldn't let each other have fun going to a coffee shop while I wanted to visit Rembrandt's house or other things like a push and pull and shove where everything you do from now on becomes a compromise of the things I wanted to push and pull it didn't take long for us to figure out that maybe we made a mistake living and doing all these things together in our homes and we were two very different characters he studied literature I did economics you fry burgers in the morning person he worked best at after 20:00 and annoyed me terribly with his typing throughout the night whenever I tried to get some sleep but I got my revenge in the morning after I brushed my teeth I would put the toothbrush in the glass but he would leave it on the stand when I wanted to do the dishes right after we had eaten he wanted to wash them later you wash them because you have to have blue eyes and light skin he laughed at me sometimes in the summer because I looked like a gypsy when I was tanned before realizing the things matter in time and they get to you sooner or later to judge them from the outside no matter how educated you are you can't see them or don't understand why you want to strangle the guy next to you when you come home and see the dishes unwashed for days when you'd say that's perfect right in the relationship looking for things you can't find in yourself and I couldn't find myself in this man not a single thing together against the whole world and a worm was chewing us from the inside and we didn't even know it how I was turned into an ugly rose eaten by worms and Solitude but beauty is just another word for pride and prejudice carried against me for getting fatter and pimples and tanned but it's good because all stories end like death and I feel words pouring out of me like my beauty and joining the beautiful river flowing like my greatest desire to become in the end a letter in a book that goes on and on and on and on and on and on and on and on."

E arlier on, I said I was not planning to work too hard this semester but I managed to pull an all-nighter just to get the schoolwork out of the way. Someone I knew liked to study at night. He said that was the only way he could really focus. He saw me online on Facebook and said I should take the first train and go for some cheap dim sum.

Just one railway station away, I reached a market. Hong Kong was starting to wake up and yet it was busier than Amsterdam on a sunny day. In the market, the people were setting up shop. Walking in from the city, you could smell the dried blood on the floor. Butchers with their huge cleavers were chopping up pigs, cows, birds, fish, sheep, cows. Pig heads, hung from hooks by the back of their heads like some precious museum pieces, a guy twisting the heads of chickens like he was a machine on a conveyor belt, another was slicing fish lengthwise and pulling their guts out, pork livers removed of their bile, calves skinned alive and hung on a thing that looked like a coat hanger, fresh carcasses taken off ice, fish so frozen they looked like rocks or fossils, a guy was blow-torching a pig and it smelled like human flesh, piles of freshly decapitated chicken heads nicely stacked. A beef carcass like the one painted by Chaim Soutine was thrown away somewhere in the back. And those eyes, every animal had those gigantic eyes staring at you, everything made ready for sale to feed the hungry people of Hong Kong. And the smell, could you imagine the smell? It was so strong I could taste it on the back of my tongue. And the noises – of knives being sharpened, of guts and cartilages being pulled out, of animals still alive, squeaking, oinking, or crying for help before their end – were sometimes covered by the static buzz of the lights above.

The escalators that took me to the dim sum place were just around the corner but I paused at all this death around me. Walking around the aisles of the market, much to the people's surprise because no other foreigner was walking around the place so early, was like walking around a museum of modern art. How else can you see the dominion of man over nature if not by watching him butchering animals? There were open markets in Prague, but not this big. When I was younger and walked with my mother to shop for groceries in the market, I refused to eat the food we were buying. Seeing a pig head or two looking at me from the fridge and its muscles and organs set up for display disgusted me so much I was imagining I was eating a piece of my own flesh. Now it made me even hungrier.

Upstairs, the place wasn't the cleanest in the world and the average age was sixty. Elderly people in ragged clothes, limp, disfigured, coughing a new strain of tuberculosis on the tables, were having their first (and probably last) meal of the day. You never really get to see so many old people in one place, and many of them were working still. They were the ones keeping Hong Kong Central alive. As a foreigner you hardly saw this, since you had other cool things to explore and do and everything was set up in such a way that you never got to see this side of the city because that's the way it was. People always try to show their better sides and mask the not-so-nice ones. How did these people see Hong Kong anyway?

I ordered us some food and we ate like pigs. Next to me on the shared table there was an old man disfigured by gigantic warts. Not a problem. I ordered small basket after small basket of dim sum, randomly pointing at the characters, most likely cooked from the animals I'd just seen downstairs. I never felt more alive and lucky in my life. Eating so much in front of these people, who were sometimes grouped in pairs of two or three for one small basket made everything look offensive. Half of the things I was putting in my mouth I had no idea what they were made from. Our table had more baskets and plates than all the other ones combined. But then I realized the people didn't care about me. They had other things to think about. My table was a ghost table. A woman was chopping up mounds of cabbage at an incredible speed. The guy who was making our dim sum had the thin dough in one hand and the filling in the other. With the exact same movements, he would smear the dough and clench his fist in such a way that it made a perfectly folded lump. I counted at least eight times the way he did it and everything was like a broken record. There was an empty seat in front of me. Hollowness came from a corner of the hall.

"Hello."

"Hello, Hollowness."

"Great to see you here. How's it going?"

"I'm good, I'm good. I like this place."

"Yes, I always like coming into these dingy places from time to time when you're not at home. Makes me feel more alive and lucky for the things I have."

"It sure does."

"Speaking of having, what's the deal between you and Fei-yan? Fine girl, this Fei-yan, isn't she?"

"What do you mean?"

"Somebody told me you guys are almost always together. You know, people might get the wrong idea."

"We're close."

"Maybe a bit too close?"

"I'm not sure I like where this is going."

"Even though you don't get the language, people are talking. Everyone likes to hear gossip from time to time."

"And what did you hear?"

"Nothing much, really. I thought it was nice letting you know, that's all."

"There's nothing going on. I'm just about to go. You should too."

"I hear long-distance relationships are quite a common thing these days. You even have determined and not determined long-distance, can you believe that?"

"What?"

"A determined long-distance relationship is when both parties know they will meet each other in two years or less. And the not determined one, well, you know."

"That's stupid."

"Maybe it is, maybe it isn't. But I heard you told somebody you want to come back to Hong Kong. You even wrote your university back home in Amsterdam if you can continue studying here. Too bad things didn't work out, huh?"

"Did you check my laptop?"

"No, I just hear bits and pieces from other people, I have my own things to deal with. But seriously, you have no idea how many girls you made jealous. And, you know, jealous girls are quite... unstable."

"I'm really not in the mood for this. Had a long night."

"What's the matter, did you guys fight?"

"Seriously. Shut up."

"As you wish. I only come to you as a friend. And I give

you this friendly advice. There's no point in stirring things up if you don't plan on taking things through to the next level. Some people have been trying to work her up for years, people with money, people with looks, powerful people, you name it. And then you come along and dance your way through this whole thing. Some things are better left the way there are. There is a whole market around Fei-yan. You have no idea, you're just a new-comer. Kinda ironic, isn't it?"

"Why can't you be happy for me? I don't care about your friendly advice or the other people I'm pissing off. Maybe if all of you would start treating her like a human being and not like a piece of furniture she would pay more attention to you. Bring some flowers and candy next time. Write a poem or get something from the internet and say you wrote it for her. Nothing is going on. Thanks for the breakfast."

I paid half the bill and went downstairs. The food was so heavy it made me sleepy and angry. Walking down the escalator, I couldn't stop thinking that all those animals were Fei-yan's rejected candidates being chopped off and sold in pieces. I was okay with that image. The market was already full. Everyone knows you have to come early to get fresh meat. It disappeared from the shelves faster than I could ever imagine.

"Did you ever hear about the Stockholm syndrome and what am I saying of course you didn't it's when you start liking your kidnappers that we were to one another and walking the streets of Amsterdam with heavy chains tied to each other pulling in different directions and squeezing the blood out of our wrists nailing our angel wings to the ground but neither of us had the courage to talk about it almost like a strange form of guilty masochism while we were carrying our chains in resentment and tried not to flap our wings not even when they got numb when we didn't use them enough we would just forget about them or they would wither and die like the legs of a paralyzed man as we asked too much from ourselves but we didn't actually have anybody else here worlds closing off getting to the teeny tiny thingy just me and him difference different worlds different sheep and roses they don't get along well together we have to get out seeing a person for too long can make your rose sick then the sheep left I was alone until I met you and I don't like you then I have to ask if I like being alone as a free young woman a free rose that can choose some writers somewhere outside my world writing my dialogue as we speak laughing about it a bit like Moses I am coming so close to the thing I want I can smell the thing I've been looking for I have one foot on The Promised Land everything just slips away where everything is clean like death and before that I was younger and didn't qualify for the national phase of the math Olympiad where they wanted me to be it was my fault for not working hard enough for not giving a hundred percent number four trophies that is what I have so far and death some people aren't meant to get the thing they want and I am okay at least I have somebody to hate for that thing where I didn't want to come to Amsterdam but I did I didn't want to be with this guy but I am rich and pretty and he is nothing like death I wanted to go to Hong Kong but instead he did go on and on and on and on and on because I don't want to make a bad image about it and did I mention he chased me for four years I wouldn't lower myself again we found ourselves wanting to escape the prison we raised around us where I prepared everything weeks ahead and he only took three hours three hours and now he's there O No Thank You I don't want to leave this house and Solitude and Moses they are alone and by now I forgot how happy I was when he left denying everything I was crying and I felt like death but we written out entirely hard for me to describe I was sad and relieved at the same time my left eye was sad because I didn't like living with him I don't like living with you but I got used to it and once you get used to something it doesn't matter so much whether you like it or not I was alone I could pee with the door open and put the dishes the way I wanted to like the city that changed once he left I will not see him or talk to him and the city again but our stories are so knotted to one another heavy the chains we grounded ourselves with his story after all where he has to talk about all the crazy things he does in Hong Kong and the exotic women he's banging and where to put Carina in all this sea of foreign vaginas and the story goes on and on and on and has to be some equality in this whole story because Carina needs to be strong so feminists can relate Carina to a moment where Carina needs to break free through her own strengths she needs to prove she can be happy without him like she promised the things Carina did after he left was to show all of that despite his devastating leave she can still find her way back to the hell where I focus on the bad things so much that remember I said I stored everything I had for him somewhere in the future when I helped him turn into what he is me dressing and undressing his socks and scratching his hairy legs as we explored Amsterdam I showed him places and traveled together but traveling is stupid like I taught him how to talk to people and how to be on his best behaviour then kiss him on his lips because he learned to ride a bike at the age of twenty years old we both knew that social skills were what can I get you save for things and take you places in the first class say Thank You Madam Thank You Sir but that doesn't even matter right now madam and sir how can I satisfy you once and for all many nights in a row where all these things went and how did we end up behaving like two autistic persons with these things in their larger schemes are only a drop in a bitter green tea served for Jan watching me swallowing my every word like tea pursed your lips I said 'bitter green tea' evaporate yourself in the words I'm saying to you but you have to see that there is hardly any tea left for you do to sip with that noise I hate everyone who reads or sees this story will notice how you try to change by listening to what I am saying but you don't even I don't see what is so special about you Jan and you have to understand there is no future for us in this story that will set us free when I rejected every crappy advance you made in the club and yet still had you come to my place the way I was hurled myself into his character maybe that dedication you have for chasing the perfect burger I've given you something else to chase around in his story you're nothing like him nothing like the guy who wrote the lines for you but I've planted some seeds inside like you would plant a baby in my uterus if you didn't use a condom don't panic you are becoming paranoid and you're wondering if that was tobacco you actually smoked while I cleaned myself from the smell of sex I don't like the smell of sex everywhere in my bed not because I wanted it but because someone else decided it beforehand it made things easier for your candle-like fire coming towards an end to do now once you've heard the story of my ex just fade off and let the others know you've gone to chase your dream of opening your own Burger Bar when your interest both in doing me and hearing my stories are no longer there what are you doing nothing but a puppet that came in right at the end of things he doesn't know what to do with me anymore since I've already fulfilled my part in all of this and you're here to move things forward for my help me while he's out there banging exotic women like me only about to run away as fast as I can before it's too late for us who are *here* we are *now* breathing through the pores of the paper or encrypted in a binary code or whatever it is they use these days for electronic versions of stories we have to realize that *life is something stupid and then you die* for the greatest mystery of human life alongside human beings is giving everything up for a kingdom not of this world belonging to Christ knew what he had in mind when he said that and maybe that where all his teachings concentrate in *my kingdom is not of this world* the meaning of this is rather simple it just has a moral dimension to it like most of the people you're going to meet Jan will live their lives not knowing what that teaching actually meant and will seek not to trouble anyone unlike other people who understand what the sentence means will *consciously seek* not to trouble themselves by imitating most men for strength that imitation in Asian cultures where some men are crushed by the teaching's meaning and die holding onto the sorrow of wanting more and having it to renounce it some years later for these people life is a continuous grinding of the teeth despite how I feel right now passing by the place I'm getting close to the more I want but I'm going to have to give it up in a couple of pages down the road when I was in Prague not so long ago there was this man who looked like Kafka do you even know what Kafka looks like guarding a door to a house I didn't know what was in that house but I knew I had to get in to get answers around though he said it's possible to go at a later time and as he was preparing to close the gate of life is something stupid and then you die before long ago I believed I have a worm inside my head who took over ever since Guy next to Solitude left me with therapy medication and seeing you his grip on me loosened over that area of my brain that is responsible for your sight it made me see this ghost Solitude itself just like you would put on some glasses that make you see certain images so the worm placed Solitude in front of my eyes next to the conversations me and the worm had stopped talking for some time now and when I failed to take my pills it too understood that it wanted too much and would later have to give it away as this story races towards the finish it too realized it was only a plague put by the writer of *our* story inside my head to give me depth as a character when Solitude was the only one that didn't understand this and decided to stay by my side but it's okay it doesn't talk too much except that time I was thinking of myself just like any other human being and that drove me crazy for you being bothered to understand that you don't belong here with a character who is never decided on what she wants at any given time how can you deal with someone who wants to curse the man who left her and the next minute offer yourself to him like some cheap whore you meet me in real life the guy who made Carina is crippled by the smallest of decisions and it shouldn't even matter in the end all that you do is only preparing for the other worldly kingdom of heaven wandering to and fro snarling and fawning at people cursed with this mixture of aggressiveness and insecurity the material of all good women never wanting to rest accusing my ex for being stupid for thinking things too much before getting anything done but it turned out he was the axis of this whole story the foundation on which everything you see was built and I was but the worm inside *his* head cursing and spitting him every chance I'd get him snarling and pointing out everyone else's horror but mine or his sealing himself off like that drove me insane and he once read somewhere that I'm like a gargoyle-head grinning on the prow of an old ship during all its voyages after all the cargo the ship carried along the distant corners of the world after the ship sank and rested on the bottom of the sea the gargoyle would still be grinning forever or until some fish decided to make it their nest when that's not all for a character to be remembered for *everything* but in the end you can grab only so much meaning before people read you and dissect you like the animal you are naked in front of everyone and they expect you to enjoy what lies behind the line you just said meanings teachings can be interpreted from everything you do every struggle is only for others not for you Jan your kingdom is not of this world who would want to write about such a complicated character like I need to get away from my purpose to let Solitude take me into *his* story which turned out to be *their* story *our* story."

S uddenly, a knock on the door. I was getting ready to finish my reading, send the papers and get some sleep before going to class. But the knock was persistent, disrupting the buzz of my air-conditioner. Lots of stories begin with a knock. This was one of them. I opened it. The lights of the hallway were off. Outside my door, Fei-yan.

"Can I come in?"

"Sure, what's wrong?"

"Nothing."

"What if I was sleeping?"

"You were not. You checked your Facebook ten minutes ago."

Fei-yan stepped inside. She stood there, looking around while I typed. She wore a hair clip with a red rose made from thin sheets of plastic.

"Somehow I imagined your room with lots and lots of books lying around like every other literature student does."

"Guess I don't need that many. I'm doing nature a favour."

"I do not like reading from a computer screen, it hurts my eyes. Nothing compares to reading a real book, holding it and smelling it. I like the smell of new books. I hate borrowing them from the library. Too many people have touched and smelled them."

"Everyone must make some sacrifices."

I turned back to my laptop. The air-conditioner made the silence between us scary. Fei-yan was still standing and looking around.

"Why do you keep your closet door open?"

"I don't know."

"It is nicely organized. I like that. My closet is not as nice as yours."

"I don't know why I do it. Guess it shows I have nothing to hide."

I paused, trying to figure it out myself.

"Did you notice that in the Netherlands they don't draw the curtains over their windows at night?"

"Really?"

"Weird, right? You can't imagine how many times I caught people in some private moments. You just walk back home from the supermarket and then, bam! An old naked guy is watching television. Or there was this other time when I saw a kid pulling his pants down and staring at his erect thing. He was completely fascinated by it. And I was too. But then, when his mother came, it got a bit awkward. Also, the mirror from my closet door fell off. I need to talk to the janitor one of these days. It's on the desk for now so I can look at myself when I work."

"Silly people," Fei-yan laughed trying to mask her uneasiness. "I always pull the curtains in my room, even though I live high up. You do not know who might be watching." She smiled before saying, "Maybe perverts like you!"

"Oh, come on! It was out there, how could I not see it?"

"I was joking. I hope I did not offend you."

"I was joking too."

"Now you are making fun of me."

"Maybe."

I looked at Fei-yan trying not to laugh. Hollowness was in bed, trying to get some sleep.

"Why are you still standing?"

"Because you did not say I could sit somewhere."

"You can sit on my bed. I need to finish this and then we can talk."

"Really? I can sit on your bed?"

"Not everyone has a bed other people should not touch, Fei-yan. I don't have any tea or sweets for you. I don't get many visitors."

I pulled the blanket away and made Hollowness find a spot on the floor. It mumbled something but in the end it moved. Fei-yan sat on the bed with her back against the wall.

"It is alright."

"What?"

"The tea. I am sure it is worse than the one I gave you. A Chinese saying goes: 'Life is too short for drinking bad tea.'"

"Really?"

"Joking!"

"I just want to talk to you."

"Okay, what do you wanna talk about?"

"Nothing. Just talk."

"Well, we can't just talk for the sake of talking. We have to talk about something."

"Like what?"

"I don't know. What was the last thing you read tonight?"

"I finished reading *Love in a Fallen City* by Eileen Chang a fourth time. Do you remember her? The Chinese writer?"

"Yes."

"In that story, there is a scene, the main characters, a guy and a girl, go to an old wall in Hong Kong, somewhere in Repulse Bay. There is a nice contrast between life and death there as the girl presses her face against the wall. And then the guy thinks about the end of human civilization. He says that after everything is destroyed, collapsed and ruined, maybe this wall will still be there. If, by some miracle, they still meet at that wall, he says, 'You will honestly care about me, and I will honestly care about you.' That wall is still there. We should go there sometime and you can buy me a cup of coffee."

I jumped off my chair and landed next to Fei-yan in bed. She was taken by surprise but didn't move away.

"So, you like playing games?"

"What do you mean?"

"Why do people need the end of the world to be honest with each other?"

"I do not know; I guess it is more romantic that way. Think about the people who are very sick and they know they are going to die. The things they say are much more important than a person you see every day."

"I'm still not convinced."

"The moments where you know something is about to end – those are the moments where you truly reveal yourself."

"So until then you're just playing a game?"

"Everyone plays it."

We stood in silence for a moment. Hollowness was grumpy. It couldn't sleep. The buzz of the air-conditioner irritated me. But I couldn't turn it off.

"I might not have the tea, but do you want to listen to some music?"

"Sure."

"You know Bob Dylan?"

"I heard about him."

I gasped and opened my mouth.

"You mean you haven't listened to Bob Dylan? No way!"

"No."

"You have no idea what are you missing. His lyrics are pretty cool. Definitely check him out."

"Let us hear it, then."

The album I played was *Blonde on Blonde*. Fei-yan wasn't so impressed by the music, and it somehow drifted into the background. I tried telling her about the lyrics, how "she" is sometimes replaced with "you" in the live versions of another album, his political affiliations, how praised it was by the critics, how *Blonde on Blonde* was one of the first double albums in history, but it didn't matter.

"Do you have someone you honestly care about?" Fei-yan asked.

"I don't know, I guess. Myself, maybe."

"Apart from that."

"But what does honestly care about mean?"

"You know what I am talking about."

"I wanted to make sure. There was this girl I thought I cared about, but it didn't work out very well."

"Yes?"

"But that is a story for another time. Let's just say I cared about her too much for both of us."

"What did you like most about that girl? Is her name Carina?"

"Yes, she's Carina. What I liked the most, I think it was the way we were so different. She was doing economics and I did literature. She is a morning person, I am not. She always has a plan, but I am, as she called it, a drifter. There were all these things we could teach each other and it was hard to get bored. But somehow we did get bored and somehow we managed to keep it together for way longer than it was supposed to be."

"Maybe the difference broke you up. I would not like somebody different from me. I see you in me and you see yourself in me. People get closer that way. If there is no chemistry, then how are you going to have a relationship?"

"It's not about being similar and different. When you have a longer relationship, you'll see that good and bad or similar and different are not so distinct. You know about this, they tell you everywhere. You'll see that some people just look for a bad guy even when he isn't there. And once you have this idea in your head, it's very easy to blame that person. Some girls just want to be treated that way."

"Are you a bad guy?"

The next song was *Visions of Johanna*. But neither of us was paying attention to what was on. Hollowness listened to the tunes and watched us with great interest, as if witnessing a play with background music.

"And what do you do with people you care about?"

"Are we playing 21 questions?"

"You do not have to answer, it is fine."

"I take care of the people I care about. I comfort them, I do things for them and with others I can even make love."

It was Fei-yan's turn to be surprised.

"You made love?"

"Yeah, a couple of times."

"Who?"

"Some girls."

Shock.

"More girls?"

"Yeah."

"How many?"

"I'm not going to tell you how many!"

"Why?"

"Because it's personal? And I don't want to brag about it."

"Sometimes I believe guys make love just to brag about it. So brag away."

"I guess I'm one of those guys who doesn't brag."

"How many?"

"Nope."

"How many? Tell me."

"I'll never tell. That way you'll have something to think about."

"Did you use a condom?"

"Yep. Not all the time."

"Do you like condoms?"

"No, not so much. Can't feel a thing."

"But why do you do it if you do not feel it?

"I don't know, it's fun."

"I used to hand out free condoms. I volunteered for something that fought against STDs."

"That's nice. And ironic."

"Why?"

"Because you never did it."

"But I want people to be safe and healthy."

"A noble goal, I'm sure of it."

"What is the difference between making love to someone and having sex?"

"Why are you so curious about sex all of the sudden?"

"I am curious about many things, you know. We do not talk much about these things in China, and you seem very experienced. But if you want to stop, then it is fine with me."

"Don't make me blush."

"Is it wrong to talk about these things?"

"No."

"Can I talk about these things with you?"

"I guess, we were doing just fine until now."

"You brought it up. I thought we were doing fine as well."

Short break.

"So what is the difference between making love and having sex?"

"For some people the two are the same," I said resuming my connoisseurship. "But for this person right here," I said pointing both of my index fingers towards me, "They are different."

"How?"

"You see, I have a theory. You make love discriminately and fuck indiscriminately."

"Yes?"

"Men and women, they are different. At least when it comes to sex. For men, it's mostly about the act itself, you know, penis + vagina = love, but for women, at least some women, I must talk like an educated person now, it's more about the intimacy. Guys just want to get it on each time they get the chance, but girls, you know, they tend to select things. Again, maybe not all of them, but you get the point. And so, I have a pretty low standard when it comes to fucking somebody else, but, you know, I only made love (as cheesy as it sounds) with three or four girls or young women, whatever you want to call them."

"That is slightly harsh."

"That's the way it is. You'll know what I'm talking about later."

"Did you love the girls you made love to?"

"Of course, that's why it's called 'making love.'"

"What is love?"

"Seriously? Are we in the first week of university where we talk about big things?"

"You do not have to answer. It is fine. Pardon my curiosity. I did not mean to go this far and I am sorry if I made you say some things you did not want to say."

I got up and poured myself some water.

The harmonica melted into our conversation. I got back onto the bed.

"These things don't work with me, Fei-yan, acting all innocent. And it's fine. I'll tell you what love is. There is this French saying, '*Le mariage est comme une forteresse assiégée, ceux qui sont dehors veulent y entrer, ceux qui sont dedans veulent en sortir.*' Do you know what it means?"

"I would imagine something about marriage?"

"Yes. In English it says, '*Marriage is like a fortress besieged: those who are outside want to get in, and those who are inside want to get out.*'"

"But why do you talk about marriage? People do not get married because they love each other. That is a recent and possibly a Western thing. Marriage used to be something that ensured the prosperity of the family."

"Just let me finish."

"Yes?"

"I'm not talking about marriage, I was just showing off my French. I don't know the marriage part, I've never been married, but love is also like a fortress besieged. It's about being vulnerable. Tearing down the fortress, you expose yourself to another person, you're at the mercy of the other."

"Do you like the music?"

Hollowness nodded.

"I was not paying too much attention. I am sorry."

"Don't be. One day you'll maybe listen to the album again and think about our talk right now and you'll thank me."

"Why?"

"Because the music fits."

Silence for a couple of minutes more. Hollowness was still watching us and it was growing impatient. Something had to happen sooner or later. The moon peered out from behind the giant tower blocks. A large white moon on a sky that was calm. No stars were visible. The moon's rays were reflected by the water, and then once more in the mirror on my desk, turning it into a shimmering pond. Bob Dylan was still on.

"Do you honestly care about me?" Fei-yan asked.

"Well, we're just going to have to wait until the end of civilization to find out."

"What would you do to me if I told you I honestly care about you?"

"I don't know, things."

"Like what?"

Fei-yan changed the tone of her voice. It was lower, almost whispered. Her tongue made a small snap on the "t" in the "what" like a gentle whip. It drove me crazy.

"Are you trying to turn me on?"

"Maybe. Why?"

The "why" was pronounced almost like a wheeze. Bob Dylan was still on.

"What would you do to me?"

"Now you're just teasing. Why?"

"Tell me, what would you do? Indiscriminately or discriminatingly?"

"Are you sure you haven't done this before?"

"What is wrong with a bit of teasing?" she said in a serpent's voice.

"I don't like being teased."

"You do not like having fun?"

I didn't reply. Hollowness didn't even blink.

"Fine, if I am such a tease, then I will just leave." Her voice turned back to normal.

She moved away from the bed and walked towards the desk and door. But then, I walked back behind her. I had one hand on her head, and with the other, I turned Fei-yan around towards me and kissed her mouth. This was the first time we did it, but it didn't feel like the first time for either of us. I thought about it, dreamt about it, replayed it in my head. Her fortress besieged. There were many times, many chances, and maybe this might have happened sooner, but neither of us dared risk it, we were that smart at the game. But now, my lips pressed against hers, she abandoning herself to me, both of us. Fei-yan pressed herself against the mirror, feeling its cold surface. Fei-yan's body shivered as I reached under her tank top, feeling her skin, learning about her the way a blind man would. I pushed her towards the mirror even more, and the shimmers of the mirror were like on a pond and both of us fell inside it, into another world where sensations bounced from love to hate to lust, to hot, cold, then red again. Fei-yan, me, our kiss, they started spinning and took the room along with it in a vortex bigger than Jupiter's Great Red Spot. I couldn't hear the music anymore.

When our lips parted, everything returned to normal. Fei-yan mumbled, "I have to go," and quietly ran upstairs. The sensor-triggered lights were off. No girls were allowed on the boys' floor after 11 PM. After I closed the door behind her, I looked at Hollowness and innocently asked, "What?" It resented me.

J an's mind was searing. He wasn't sure if it was because he had to go to work soon and grill his burgers or because of the story he just heard. Nevertheless, everything Carina said was now stored up or better said locked away somewhere inside his brain – it was a takeaway. She was silent in the corner and stared at me, Solitude. There were some birds chirping after the rain. The light crept slowly into Carina's room, over her library and table, uncovering a night of decadence and pleasure. Carina told her story because she cared about Jan, even though she didn't like him. But all Jan could think about was how he would not call her again. He looked again at the clothes on the floor, on the furniture and books that had their titles barely visible. Carina was silent and Jan took her silence as an excuse for looking around. Jan stretched his arms and back. What the hell was he doing here in the first place? What was going to happen with them? The story he just heard hung around his neck like a noose. He had to leave soon but something kept him. He was expecting something like a climax, like an explosion of colour or something, but she said this was the last night they would spend together and he was disappointed by this "ex." Carina's flesh was still soft but all Jan wanted to do was to bike to work and think about burgers and stories of distant places. He didn't like seeing Carina in the early morning. She was exhausted and had dark circles under her eyes. Her hair was messed up and some blackheads had made their way onto her nose. The room was colder.

But then Jan of the Burger Bar, looked around again. Everything seemed changed or out of place. Carina's room seemed borrowed from a movie décor. The walls were numbered not four, but three. He could distinguish some cameras somewhere in the distance, pointing at different angles and what he thought was the light of the sun was nothing more than some powerful reflectors. He left Carina, put his underpants on and walked around. The walls were made of cardboard and they were supported by some wooden pillars. Jan tried shaking the walls off the pillars but they were too heavy. What had happened? He was sure he was somewhere in Amsterdam East. How could he now be on a movie set? Where was the exit? He had to go to work soon. What was the time? Outside the room was dark but

Jan could feel that the space was much larger than the room itself. He tried running outside but no matter how fast he ran, he couldn't move away from the furniture. It was as if he was dragging it after him just like he had to drag along the story Carina had been telling him all night. Running around back to the set, Jan saw Carina nodding to a figure sitting in one of the corners of the room. It was disgusting and Jan couldn't even look at its face – he could only see the ragged shirt it was wearing and the thin long hands that looked infected with leprosy. Carina was also out of bed. She was still naked. "We have to go. Are you ready?" Then the monster grabbed Carina and jumped with her out of the window. It didn't make any sense, but Carina fell down. Jan could see her legs were twisted in an unnatural position, her back crushed and a small red puddle behind her head. Jan tried jumping out of the window as well but he was still on the same level as Carina's studio. Jan couldn't breathe. Those leprous hands grabbed him by the neck, crushing his windpipe. Jan's heart was beating faster and faster and he tried to take a look into the eyes of the thing that was squeezing the life out of him before rolling up his eyes, and becoming one with the darkness around Carina's room. ******

"Were you sleeping?"

Jan opened his eyes all of a sudden and saw Carina in bed next to him. He touched his face, then he touched Carina's. Everything seemed to be in order.

"Yeah, I was just resting my eyes before work. Your coffee is not as strong as it used to be. I had a very strange dream. It was..."

"I don't want to hear your dream," Carina interrupted him. "Talking about dreams kills them. That's why they're called dreams – they're fiction."

They stayed for another couple of seconds in silence. Jan's legs were beginning to sweat under the blanket. The sun was already up and he needed to go back to work.

"Do you have a place to stay?"

"Yes. Why?"

"Do you mind if I wait there until you come back from work? I can't stay here anymore. I won't see him again. Me and my ex, we're never going to be together in my room, our room. There's no point in keeping this door open."

"Sure. It is possible."

"I'm going to Macau," she said. "Crazy spontaneous decision." Fei-yan decided it was best to let me know before she disappeared for a couple of days. Who with? I wasn't supposed to know. Fei-yan could always come to my place and every time I would be there, but I couldn't reach *her* if I wanted to. It all had to do with the power game we were playing. There were all these people around Fei-yan, people who were nameless and faceless to me and I didn't know which one it was.

I found out it was another guy. Of course, most people would have some sort of reaction, right? Like anger, confusion, possibly even a desire for revenge. How could she act like that? How could she do that, what was she thinking? I felt nothing. I said nothing tied us, we were just looking for comfort and taking advantage of each other; so good for her. After all, no one is irreplaceable, but what if? What if she did this as a test of faith? Weird things happen. You don't know why, but they do. And it's best not to talk about them. It's best if you never talk to people you were once very attached to. Ever. It's like one of those books you only read once and that's it. Close it, put it in your library, and then leave it there until it becomes valuable at auctions.

Fei-yan wasn't my girlfriend. I could picture her putting on a nice dress and make-up, maybe a hat and sunglasses, but no, she didn't wear hats. And then Fei-yan and I were sitting by the ferry terminal for Macau, and she would say to me, "It is because you do not expect anything from people, that is why I am doing this," and then she would give her arm to some random guy with a face as flat as the space between a doll's legs and walk onto the boat. "I am not like that," she would say as the ferry prepared to leave. "I am not like you, I have expectations of people and I want to see if they are correct." And then I would stay on the pier and watch her and her dress being taken away as the ferry revved up its engines and she would look like something from a different world, a sort of charming, long-lost and fucked-up kind of grace you don't see any more. She wouldn't look back at me through her window even though she had a seat by it. But I did. I watched her for a very long time, staying there still like time.

Watching her getting smaller and smaller and watching as

the ferry raced through the small islands and the people pushing me back to the waiting area, time slowly picked up the pace. On her side, I would become smaller and smaller, like a dot, and she would see Hong Kong sinking. After ten minutes or so into the ride, the skyscrapers were the last things that could be seen, with their tips and antennae reaching outwards and in the end, Fei-yan, the ferry, her departure, seemed never to have existed in the first place.

I woke up from trying to realize the things happening with Fei-yan and random guys, in the same daze as I would wake up in from a scary and violent dream. I consoled myself saying the logic of someone like her couldn't be subjected to any form of reasoning, always blaming it on the Other.

Who in their right mind would do that? I guess some things don't change. Why should I? This story could have been one about redemption, about this guy who goes to Hong Kong and finds something else there, learns, completes a pilgrimage and returns better than the man he was when he left Amsterdam and Carina (Carina!). And then, at the end of everything, dreams, loss, adventures would melt into the painful bitter-sweetness I loved so much. I could've been many things in this story, I could've been the money-spending tourist in Hong Kong where my biggest adventure would be where to get smashed next, I could've met exotic Asian women and had sex with them, I could've had enlightening experiences like all foreign travelers. I could've taken lots of pictures. But this story is not about Hong Kong, not even about change or becoming. It's about how things *don't* change. The city, the landscape, it doesn't matter. It could have been any city, and I would still have run around chasing the same thing and I don't even know what it is. Here I am, at the end of the world, almost finishing this journey, this pilgrimage but I open the same doors and I'm telling that single story all over again.

For now, a loneliness I could not write about. Colours would just splash one onto another, cancelling each other out and the end result was just black and I cannot understand why. I always thought it strange in my middle school when you mix too many colours during the arts class, they'd turn black no matter what. And once you'd reach that black, the colour (most likely a bright one, like yellow or white) would be compromised. I was one of those colours. Seeing Fei-yan leave meant that everything turned into that black milk of daybreak I could no longer escape from.

The day when I saw her message dragged on forever, for this had truly happened, and I was abandoned in this big city with no eyes, mouth or ears.

She was going to be back in a couple of days. Fei-yan's image would always be right next to this place, to Hong Kong, and I couldn't picture them apart. Her leaving was my leaving. We armed ourselves with giant hammers and smashed down the walls of our fortress in the bliss of mutually assured destruction. Was that change?

Buzzing away with the giant diesel engines in a ferry with some random guy I would never know or see. A world where we were no longer able to share the small thing we had. There are key moments in life where, for a short while, the true self reveals itself to you. Most of the times we're not aware of it because we're too busy to share pictures over Facebook and Whatsapp and talk non-sense all day. But every hair strand of my hair, every pore and every cell electrified whenever I got close to Fei-yan and announced that *I* was there. But seeing her off in my dream, that buzz was over.

I had no idea how to get it back. My real departure would come a bit later, but I wondered if this was the way things were supposed to be. Going back to Amsterdam, doing the coursework, cooking simple meals and getting high and/or drunk once in a while. You know, that same kind of routine that makes the days pass on like the flow of sand through a narrow tube.

But with that dream of mine, going back to Amsterdam meant that other people would look for change in me. On the outside, nobody would notice it: I still have more or less the same weight, my hair has grown, and that was about it. Black is nice. People who mourn wear black. People who have something taken away from them forever wear black. I like wearing black.

I couldn't care less what Fei-yan and the random guy were doing in Macau. Like Ulysses waking up from Calypso's bed, but then getting back in, like a hand or a foot waking up from numbness before going numb again, change passed by me as you finished reading this sentence. I owed something to Fei-yan. Then we would have shared maybe another secret, another invisible threat.

Some of the people I knew were going out that night.

I know that strange coincidences are a common trick, especially when writing things, but I really got lucky that night. As a person, or maybe as a character, I never claimed I can get any girl I want or that I know how to make girls jealous so that they could like me more. More often than not, I'm the jealous and insecure guy. Accumulated, my experience with girls isn't that great. I don't know the rules of the game, what are the hints, or anything like that. I know I secretly threatened Fei-yan to do something bad myself (but good and bad aren't the terms I would like to use here, as if there is a clear distinction), but I had no idea where to start. I just thought I would get drunk and call it a night, like most of my nights out in Hong Kong.

But for some reason, I scored. I wasn't looking for it or anything, but things have a strange way of coming to you when you don't look for them. I tried to remember her name so I can write it down, but I couldn't. I think she didn't, either. Too hard to pronounce. She came to me as I was hanging around in some club in Hong Kong Island. It had it all: Glances thrown across the room, closely getting together, exchanging names yelling in our ears, the places where we were from, and slowly proceeding to make out on the dance floor as the bass rumbled in our stomachs. All this time I was laughing at myself for going through such an embarrassment and wondering if I would really share the cab home with this girl. It was just like in the movies or a music video. Guy sees girl dancing in the club, he takes her home and gets laid. As the songs went on and the club was beginning to empty, I'd get the feeling we understood each other. I saw her face from time to time as the strobes filled the club with light, and she wasn't that bad. She was, though, going back and forth inside her head, thinking if she would go all the way and change this thing into a clearly defined form of sin. But the music was so loud we couldn't exchange many words, but we did exchange saliva and lips and tongue and gums.

I read once in a book that whenever Chinese girls are interested in you there is a very obvious slowing of their usual quickness of movement. But she didn't seem slow to me. In fact, she was rushing things through. At some point she said she was going to leave. I followed her to the exit and grabbed her hand.

She looked at me, she looked at her hand, and in that flash of a strobe, the deed was done.

"Where?" she asked me.

"We can try going to my room," I said.

Sharing the cab with her and her two other friends (it was cheaper that way) was awkward. For one thing, they didn't say a word for the whole ride, and second, I tried making some conversation with the girl I was about to sleep with, but all I got were very plain, sometimes rude one-line answers.

The taxi dropped us off and she waved goodbye to her friends. We didn't say a word as we walked up to where I lived. Fortunately, the guard was sleeping and he was too dizzy to come chase us as we ran up the stairs to my floor. Taking the elevator would have been way riskier for us. She was impressed by the number of papers on my desk and asked if I was a writer or something. I jokingly said I was and I asked her if she wanted something, like water or tea. The way she was sitting on my bed with her legs crossed and her handbag still on her shoulder required a bit of atmosphere. Girls have this way of communicating things. So I turned off the lights and pulled the curtains back. The sun was almost rising. I wanted to put some Bob Dylan on, but then I figured she might not like it, so in the end there was no music. She put the handbag on the chair and I took off my jacket.

We simply went at it. As the night went on in a straight-forward manner, so did this, like one of those other nights where you fuck indiscriminately. Sex, a bit of rest, and that was it. Who was this girl, what was her story, why did she come all over my bed, that was unnecessary.

Hollowness was taken by surprise when I rushed into my room with a girl and in the heat of the moment, it jumped out of the bed. She stayed on the floor for the whole night watching two people doing it as if it was the most normal thing in the world. Porn works in the same way, I guess.

She wanted to sleep (was I that good?) after the thing was done. I couldn't. I was sticky, sweaty and ashamed. Both of us, naked in my bed, next to a body we knew but at the same time foreign. Her breath was calm. The buzz of the air-conditioner, cooling us off, turned into the most nerve-wracking noise I had ever heard. I reached over and tried to find my phone on the desk, tapping the wooden ledge. Maybe if I could just reach it, I could check my Facebook, and the time until she got dressed and left would pass easier. Why was she so quiet? A while ago she was screaming in a language I couldn't understand and my only concern was about my neighbours and the thin walls between us. Her calmness, her comfort in being naked next to this guy she knows almost nothing about, terrified me. I scratched my abdomen, and the rustling sound sent wave after wave of painful impulses. I was slowly losing my mind. I didn't think about Fei-yan, I was just ashamed of myself.

Hard as they were, the hours passed. We did it again shortly after she woke up, but it wasn't as good as before. She put her dress on, searched for her handbag, and I saw her off at the entrance to my dorm. I waved to the guard as I took the elevator to my floor. Fei-yan was supposed to come back in a couple of days.

I looked for Fei-yan the whole day. Nothing. Her phone was off and she was not at her place. I chatted with other people, asking them if they had seen her – nothing. Fearing another day of becoming a ghost, I stood in my room doing almost nothing. I only got out to get something to eat and take a shower. Hollowness waited.

It was close to midnight when somebody knocked on my door. Fei-yan was outside, asking if she could come in. "Of course, of course, come on in." There was nobody else in the hallway. As usual, she sat on my bed with her back against the wall. She took my pillow and rested it on her legs.

"How's it going?"

"I'm alright."

"I looked for you the whole day."

"I know. Some people told me you did."

"Where were you?"

"Out."

"Out where?"

"I saw my best friend off at the airport. She left for Europe and I do not know when I will see her again."

I sat next to her.

"Funny how things change around you, isn't it?"

"I am graduating this semester too. And then what?"

"I don't know. You'll think of something."

"You are leaving tomorrow."

"I know."

She paused for a moment. Her fingers were drawing patterns on my pillow. She did that whenever she had something to say.

"Funny to watch people leave you. You get an immediate sense of pain like you would when you witness a terrible crime. Going forward, you learn to accept that people come and go. Easy come easy go. If there is anything I would wish or pray for it would be *time*. The kind of time that comes and goes over and over again. Once you pass a certain age you are frustrated for not finding the lost time because something called life gets in the way. All great heroes need to grow up and get a decent job. I wish I did not have four hundred months to find someone to whom I can trust my babies. Even in this city, which I hate, everything would be so much better if I could graduate now and then start over again. Going there but coming back here now and again. But I have passed that stage and I do not know how many months I have left. But I am getting there. Sometimes slower, sometimes faster, but I am going in that direction. The people who leave me, they show me I am going, racing towards those months, and when I finish them, it will be too late. You see, you told me by the steps some time ago that you feel like a terminally diseased patient, but in reality, *I* am the patient. I cannot take it anymore. I cannot take it anymore."

She started crying. The same silent cry that melted the insides of my chest. Consistent, almost metronomic. Somehow I couldn't picture her crying otherwise. I took her in my arms and waited for her tears to quiet down. In the meantime, I thought about something to say, something inspiring. But no matter what I said, I would be lying. Fei-yan leaned towards me and kissed my neck, and my shirt and pillowcase were spotted with her tears, her warm breath. I kissed her forehead. Trembling, her hand grabbed one of my shoulders and squeezed. Her other hand took the collar of my shirt, pulling me down. I took her by the waist. Fei-yan put the pillow in its usual spot, then she pulled me onto the pillow alongside with her. The moment her head touched the pillow I coiled myself around her. I kissed her neck, her eyes, her cheeks, and the backs of her ears. My hands and lips walked along Fei-yan's clavicle and sternum while my other was wandering on her lower back. Mapping the places I already knew, finding comfort in the regions I explored, going on expeditions to places I wasn't granted access to before, testing the waters, squeezing here and there and waiting for responses. I couldn't even tell what Fei-yan was doing – if she did something in the first place. Why did she wait for so long?

I took my time undressing her – you always have to take your time in the beginning. She didn't say anything as I took her tank-top down and her shorts. She would sometimes flinch and get goose-bumps, only to relax in a surrendering tenderness. Her eyes, pointing towards me, were sometimes asking me, "What are you doing, what are you doing, what are you going to do with me?" But then, answering herself, she kissed me on the neck. Just like with the pillow, her fingers would make unknown patterns on my back and at times, as if she had drawn something wrong, she would sink her nails in as if the drawings were being carved in my flesh.

I turned the lights off. Taken by surprise, Fei-yan lifted her head off the pillow. She covered herself with the blanket, which was crumpled on the other end of the bed.

I undressed and threw everything on the chair. Fei-yan was staring at the ceiling as if my body was the only thing that animated her. I couldn't see Hollowness. It was supposed to be there, watching. Fei-yan moved over so I could come in. But when I lifted the blanket, Hollowness was already there. It waved at me, but I couldn't make a scene here, not now, when I was so close. Reading my mind, Hollowness made me understand it was going to leave. But then, Hollowness became more and more transparent, and moulded itself after Fei-yan. Hollowness turned into something that sucked Fei-yan in. Just like a snake would eat its prey, Fei-yan was inside Hollowness. She didn't seem to notice she was covered in slime. There was still time to back down.

"What happened? Are you coming in?"

I was under the blanket. At first I told myself I could go through with this, it's not so bad. But after a minute or two, I was grossed out. Her hands and her breasts left small traces of goo all over me. It was like I was trying to sleep with a fish – a slimy, fresh-out-of-the-water fish. Fei-yan clutched at me.

Fei-yan grabbed my shoulders as I went inside and let out a gasp of surprise. I pushed as far as I could. This is how it must feel when you gut somebody. I stayed there for the longest time holding Fei-yan and not saying a word. We looked into each other's eyes, I, being absorbed in them, she, confused and scared in mine. The goo was thin enough to make my exploration incomplete, but I could still feel our pulses synchronizing. Fei-yan was the first one who broke off the eye contact and then all her flesh, all the tension that was inside her melted away. The air-conditioner was on so our bodies could cling to each other without sweating. I said to myself I was going to push through with or without the slime, so I did it. I waited for her to relax, then I started moving, gently, slowly, like the way you'd do it in the beginning. Towards the end, she put her arms around me, almost covering me in that goo and let a small laugh out. I couldn't tell if it was Fei-yan or Hollowness speaking. Her palms covered my ears and it was like sinking in a bathtub.

When everything was over, Hollowness resumed the spot on the floor, watching us. Fei-yan was sleeping with her back to me. I didn't know what to say or do. I wanted to take a shower, to wash all the slime off, but I was afraid she would leave by the time I got back. I watched her for a long time. Her breathing, like her crying, metronomic. I was sick to my stomach.

When I woke up, she was gone. Surprisingly how the Sun, 92,960,000 miles away, can manage a perfect headshot from that distance. The curtains were drawn and only a slit was open. And through that slit, the Sun sent yellow and purple spikes through my eyelids. Hollowness was in Fei-yan's place and was sitting in the same position. I jumped out of bed and I pulled the blanket away, but the sheets were clean. No slime, no goo, no blood. Nothing. The air-conditioner buzzed through the night. Fei-yan left a strand of hair on my pillow as a parting gift.

L ook at them getting dressed without saying a word. Carina went to the bathroom to change and to freshen up. Jan asked her if he could borrow some of her toothpaste. She put some on his finger and Jan cleaned his mouth with water. By now he was already used to Carina's disgust at morning breath. They had nothing more to say, and even if they did, it didn't matter. He tried to smile, she was numb. As soon as they got out through that door into Amsterdam's strong air, and with Solitude following them, Jan still couldn't find a way to tell her what he was thinking about so many mornings before: that it was over, pointless, that was the last time. In *How to Date Girls*, it is almost always good advice not to interrupt someone who is talking, that is why he didn't want to say it back then. Jan was polite and heard everything without seeming too bored, just like the sacred places and rituals he couldn't possibly understand but still respected.

There was nobody outside. Nobody. The sun – the real sun – crept behind some buildings. The *tabaksmagazijn* was not open. That was strange, because Jan needed some filters. How was he going to get through today? Ask for some filters from his co-worker? That could be a possibility. Still, Jan was still haunted by that dream he had had in Carina's bed. At the corners of the streets, he would look back and check if the façades of the buildings were made of cardboard or not, much to Carina's surprise. Amsterdam was an unreal city. But then Jan thought the morning wind was too strong for the cardboard so everything was alright for now. Even though he couldn't possibly understand what Carina's story meant, or maybe he was dreaming all this time, the words opened a hole in his heart. He couldn't shake off the feeling that something was wrong, that he had done things the wrong way, or maybe something else was waiting for him, something bigger. He couldn't wait to share this story about a crazy chick from Prague with someone else.

There was nobody in the station waiting for the tram. Nobody. In front of them, the tracks wound in the distance like two giant tapeworms. Jan remembered Carina saying something about worms and brains but he couldn't be bothered to remember what that was all about. He could only picture the number of orders he had to take today – and they were many. Carina caught

Jan staring at the tracks and smiled. Maybe he finally understood something.

Ding! The bell of the tram rang like a block of ice dropped to the floor. Normally, there were cars, shops opening up, bikers rushing to work and kids crossing the street, whenever Jan left Carina's early in the morning. The bell would then lose itself in the background noise, but this time is was a distinct sound that sent shivers through Jan's heart.

Solitude drove the tram and waved at Carina as it pulled into the station. Solitude liked driving trams from time to time, he even had the uniform and all. Why aren't all the tram drivers going mad rolling these metal coffins down the back of the worms? Solitude pointed at the ticket scanner. The thing beeped twice and a green light lit each time the card was placed against the scanner.

Carina and Jan were the only people on the tram. They sat in front of a screen that displayed commercials for scooter rentals, the marijuana & hemp museum, some pizza places and the Dutch national museum, the Rijksmuseum.

At the next station, so many people entered the tram that Carina and Jan couldn't breathe. They were forced to give their places to some elderly people. There were some scattered morning conversations among the persons in the tram. When somebody was talking, at least five other pairs of eyes were looking at him or her, that's how many people were inside. A middle-aged businessman was reading the newspaper on the tram – something that reminded him of the old days when people read actual newspapers. Those around him were peeking at the newspaper as well. Those who didn't have anything to read would just look around the sign-boards with advertisements or rules of good conduct. Others were just staring outside the window counting the shop signs along the street or staring into their mobile phones. They simply had to do something to fill up this loneliness. If not, then they would start thinking for themselves and everybody knows that's not good.

Carina had to do something on her own. She had thought too much after I had left and now was scared – but she didn't show any sign of this. She knew something all these faceless and nameless people didn't – that they were about to remain faceless and nameless for the rest of their days. But Carina was also proud. It was like in one of those Cold War era Hollywood movies where this one character holds the key to the whole movie, she knows how to disarm the bomb or the codes to the nuclear missiles. Only Carina could do nothing about it.

People were exiting the tram, but Solitude didn't let anyone else in. The doors were closing down in a single sweep. "Let us in!" they cried, "at least until the next stop! There are children and old people here! Please!" But the doors remained closed, no matter how many times the people pressed the button. From both sides of the glass, the people were feeding on each other's fears.

The tram already knew where it had to go. Most people got off at their stops without paying attention to the growing crowds that were waiting for a ride. Solitude was implacable. By now, the tram had cleared so that Carina could see the buildings outside. When walking around Amsterdam, it's impossible not to notice how some of the buildings, especially the old ones, are tilted. Because their foundations are built on soft ground and the buildings stand on wooden logs, it is only a matter of time before they lean as if they are trying to pick something up.

Looking out of the windows to her right and left, Carina saw the exact same thing. Buildings on both sides of the road started leaning towards one another as if they were trying to kiss. Solitude opened the driver's door and came next to Jan and Carina. Solitude extended its arms, almost touching the windows on both sides, and slowly pulled. After two or three more stops, the buildings were joined at the edges, forming an arcade that gave the impression of a tunnel. The buildings leaned so much that the shops and bakeries and pharmacies were flattened. Sewer pipes burst spewing out the waste and dirty water all over the desperate people, the iron bars of the balconies were contorted in such a way that they looked like hands trying to grip each other in an embrace that would last forever, windows cracked and sprinkled glass powder everywhere, the bridges were pressed at their highest point and, just like when you squeeze a rubber toy, they looked like a frown.

The side streets erupted in noise as trucks filled with people dressed in white descended upon the passers-by, beating them, covering them in faeces, shooting off their guns indiscriminately, rounding them up in their trucks and driving them away. Women, children, old people living in Amsterdam, everything.

The faceless and nameless people were being sealed off, taken away somewhere outside, somewhere outside this world. Families, friends, former lovers would never be seen again as the story came to its end. After all the people had disappeared, the cleaners took out huge paint guns and made everything behind the tram black. It was the same black milk of daybreak from Jan's dream, the black that turns into nothingness. There was a man who looked like Carina's ex-boyfriend in the distance. He played with his vipers his eyes were blue. He grabbed for the pen in his belt and swung it in the air his eyes were blue. He wrote as everything grew dark. He shouted, "You will all melt in this tar, you'll have a grave outside this page, where you won't lie too cramped!" The tram picked up speed and passed him. They were safe.

After a while, the bricks of the buildings were pressed so tightly to one another they were becoming a living tissue. The tunnel made by the blocks was now flesh and the tram was rushing towards the light at its end. Carina had been through this thing before. When she visited Auschwitz and saw the main entrance, she couldn't figure out what those people in the trains were thinking as they went through. From a distance, the gate's desolation was a point of rebirth. There was nothing to be done as they were rushing through the end of the story, so why bother being scared?

Among all this chaos, the tram still continued on its original route and people were getting off as if nothing happened. Carina and Jan both saw what was going on outside, but neither of them wanted to say a thing. "Aren't you bored?" Jan said, trying not to look out. "We could chat for a bit, there's no harm in that. What do you want to have for dinner?" The tram was almost empty and they were still standing very close to each other like in the beginning. Jan considered taking Carina by the waist and saying something encouraging like, "Everything will be alright." Taking all her features individually, Carina actually looked pretty. Girls are much prettier after you sleep with them.

She smiled. Until now she couldn't imagine Jan being sweet. But that was him. He was a real man from the real world with his hair smelling like grilled beef. "Don't worry. We'll figure something out," Carina replied and blushed. Jan couldn't believe he could make anyone blush. Jan was a son, a brother, a cousin, a worker at the Burger Bar, a passenger on the tram, an Amsterdammer, a horrible pick-up artist. But to this young woman, whom he just slept with and knew almost nothing about, he was a man. A real man from the real world. He wanted to know her better, they wanted to share everything there was to share but the blackness was catching up. Only they and Solitude rode the metal coffin on the backs of living worms through the uterus of Amsterdam.

"I have to get off."

Your ashen face, Carina.

"Why?"

"I forgot my bike at your place."

"Don't be stupid, I don't have a place anymore!"

"You don't understand. I have to get off. I have to bike to work."

"Don't. Don't leave me here!"

"My part in this is over. Now I have nobody to share the story with. I have to bike to work."

Carina didn't say anything. It was his decision.

"Here are my keys. You know where I live, right? I'll meet you there. Don't worry."

The tram stopped one last time and Jan got off as if nothing was wrong. Carina turned her head away as if she didn't care. The hydraulic doors were sealed shut. For her, Jan was already no more.

Ding! The tram announced its departure, passing Jan as he was trying to figure out which way to go. She looked away.

The tram picked up speed and walked along its usual route. Only she and Solitude remained. Carina went and sat on the seat behind the driver. The tram was reaching the final stop. The tram was safe. The buildings protected it.

That was it. My plane to Amsterdam was supposed to leave around midnight. I slept for a couple of hours and started packing. I had to check out of my room by 11:00. It didn't take me very long, I had few things with me. The only thing I forgot were the razors.

A human being's life is not worth as much as we like to think. Of course, you have all those people who clawed their way into history and high-school students are forced to study them, but I'm talking about the commoner: about you, about me, about *us*. Nothing and nobody is irreplaceable. The world simply moves on without you, whether you like it or not.

Something in me widens, like a void, a hole that traps everything and takes me to another place. I recognize the same lightness of being I had when I first came to Hong Kong. Maybe I just took a wrong turn on one of Amsterdam's canals biking to my place. Maybe I was going to wake up in a hospital bed with Carina by my side, her make-up all messed up and hair uncombed. How could I go back now? How to return to what I had before and how to tell anyone – even Carina – about what happened in this place I cannot understand? After I managed to get used to this place, getting used to Fei-yan and Hollowness, now I have to find my way back home (home?) or better yet, yanked back to a place that changed in my absence. Packing my clothes and books, my laptop, my music player and the small souvenirs I've gathered, pictures of Carina smiling next to me, the room looked just like any other place – hollow. Standard, like any other room in the block. Seeing the desolation – the empty shelves, the empty drawers and desk, the bed with only the mattress – it all became clear that there is nothing for me out there. Only a sense of nostalgia for something or someone or someplace that I might not end up in a second time. Few things can change the fact that I am Hollowness. I'm hollow and naked in front of the things I want. I pinched myself a couple of times while folding my clothes so that maybe – just maybe – I would wake up. It wasn't going to happen. Hollowness and I pressed against my suitcase and managed to lock it in the end.

What's with that Fei-yan girl anyway? I know I told her all these things and crossed some lines that won't be forgotten, but love? What if she was the Carina in my dream? A time might come, I said to myself, where everything would come together and I would know whether this was something else than what's been written here, but for now, my head was a blank. Nothing but emptiness and solitude. I could not picture this day coming, and yet here it is, and here I am folding my shirts mechanically and placing them in my suitcase.

There were all these small clues in my room Fei-yan was here. As much as Hollowness wanted to hide them away, I could still notice them. The hint of perfume coming back to the room after throwing away the garbage could be the aftertaste of my hand running through her hair, or it could be the barely perceivable strand of hair in front of my door like some sort of territorial marker. It was the same when I lived with Carina – perfumes, creams, stockings, tampons, a pair of slippers, the extra toothbrush. Now, all was gone.

Like the other days before, a knock on my door. Fei-yan.

She didn't sleep much. Probably she had a lot of work to do. I welcomed her in and she sat on the bed.

"This is it," she said.

"Yep. Pretty much."

"Your room is empty."

"As it should be. I'm leaving. I still have a couple more hours to go."

"I know. You can leave your suitcase in my room before you go."

"Thanks."

There we were, two people in an empty room. I could try describing how the room reflected in our souls, I could try to describe how we were crushed by an invisible weight, I could try, the way Fei-yan looked in that moment, but there was nothing. Just me, her, and Hollowness in a room that looked just like other rooms down the corridors.

"Fei-yan?"

"Yes?"

"Do you want to go on a date with me?"

She laughed.

"You want to date me?"

"You know, one last dinner together. No harm done, right?"

"You could have asked me a long time ago."

"It's more poetic this way."

"What should I wear?"

"Nothing too fancy."

We took my suitcase to her room. The elevator was packed with people taking stuff out. I said goodbye to some people I would never see again in my life and I was alright with that. By the time we reached her floor, there was nobody but me, her, the cleaning lady and Hollowness. The elevator beeped and announced the number in Cantonese, Mandarin, and finally English. The cleaning lady was on her way to inspect the rooms on Fei-yan's floor, and the three of us walked into her room together.

"You said I wouldn't step in here again."

"I could not carry your bag up here by myself. Want some tea?"

"I'm good, thanks."

"I want to take a nap. I barely slept last night. Or do you want to go now?"

"No, it's way too early. And it's raining outside."

"Thank you."

"Alright then. Guess I'll knock on your door once you wake up."

"No."

I saw Hollowness playing with the Bavarian gingerbread heart from the corner of my eye. I looked at Fei-yan as if my eyes wanted to say, "What do you want me to do, then? Stay here, watching you sleep?"

"You can nap too if you'd like."

"But your bed..."

"You can nap on the armchair."

Hollowness stood there, watching me trying to make a decision.

"Sure. Nap sounds great."

I put my suitcase down and rested my feet on it. Fei-yan stayed in her bed, watching me doing all these things. Hollowness took a shower, used Fei-yan's scrub, took the pajamas out of my briefcase and waited. Fei-yan was wearing the same white t-shirt and Hollowness was wearing my striped pajamas which looked like the ones they used to give you in death camps. She moved over and pulled aside the blanket so it could get in. Hollowness sat on the bed, wiped the soles of its feet, and got in with the same stillness and piety priests have when they put on their gowns. My heart was racing. Smiling, Hollowness took her in its arms and fell asleep. I was watching from the armchair used to greet guests. They slept with no dreams, no twitches, a sleep so deep it looked like a coma, the same sleep you would have when you return home after a long journey, the same sleep Ulysses must have had when he came back home to Penelope. I wish I could have prayed to the gods – any gods – to make the afternoon a bit longer. But I was already gone by the time I made my prayer. And so was Fei-yan.

We woke up at the same time. Hollowness was staring out of the window watching the rain.

"Do you want to do something else before we go out?"

"I would like to smoke a cigarette and see the skyline one last time."

"Where do you want to take me for our date?"

"I have nothing in mind. Take me to a place where you like eating. It's your city, after all."

"Fine."

I watched Fei-yan getting ready, putting on her make-up and choosing which dress to wear with the same focus artists have. I looked out of her window one last time, drawing in the neighbourhood over the water, with my eyes. While Fei-yan was dressing, I could have written the saddest lines. Instead, I watched her dressing up for a funeral. How couldn't I love the way she was doing things for me under my own eyes? But it came and went. She went back about her business. I washed my face, picked up my jacket, and we were ready to go.

We didn't talk in the train. What was there left to say? Our eyes would meet sometimes only to move away from each other. She grabbed my hand and twined her fingers into mine. On the opposite chair, I could see Hollowness catching glimpses of us among all the other commuters. Now I didn't have a house, so Hollowness was following me everywhere.

We got off at Tsim Sha Tsui. It was raining and I opened the umbrella for her. I took her by the waist and shared it. "Now I have a good reason to hold you," I tried joking. We walked on this large street with a lot of lights and a lot of luxury shops – *Gucci, Prada, Armani, Cartier.* Even in this rain, there were still people lining outside the shops waiting to get in. Others were looking for shelter. Hollowness was playing hopscotch, jumping from puddle to puddle, splashing the passers-by. A silence surrounded us as the rain washed off the city. The streets were sweating.

We had dim sum in a fancy place. We didn't have to wait long for a table to become free. Again, we ordered dishes, soups, dim sum, pork chops and rice, and drinks. Next to us, Hollowness was clinking wine glasses with some noisy French guys at the next table. We ate, we didn't talk, we were stuffing our faces. Good food makes us happy. I couldn't believe I was doing this. Even at that point, I was still expecting to go home with her and just meet again some other day. This whole thing was one big joke – and in a perverse way, I liked it.

"Can't remember the last time I've been on a date. Like a real date."

"Mine was two weeks ago."

"Touché."

Dishes and baskets were replaced with other dishes and baskets.

"Fei-yan?"

"Yes?"

"How are you feeling?"

The question took her by surprise. She paused for a moment and finished chewing her rice with fried shrimp.

"Numb. That is how I feel. I feel like an actor who got bored of playing the same thing for thirty years. Automatic. Numb."

I could only smile.

"I don't know, I guess I should introduce a new thing. From now on I'm going to ask girls if they want to go on a silent date with me."

She laughed – first laugh of the day.

"I only laughed because your joke was so bad. It is amusing how, even now, when you have a plane to catch, you are still making your terrible jokes. They have their humour."

"I do my best."

When the bill came, Fei-yan took her wallet out. "Don't even dare," I said. "A date is a date. You'll pay me another time." Hollowness asked me for the change to pay for the bus ride back.

We walked into the rain again. Fewer people were on the streets and holding Fei-yan by the waist under the umbrella gave me a sense of power and hope. Close to the Avenue of Stars, the place where you can see Hong Kong Island and its skyscrapers, there was a young street musician playing a very popular song. Behind him there was a huge billboard with a model in a bathing suit and the name of a popular brand.

"Hm, nice," I said.

"Back to Europe, eh? Nice girls, blond hair, long legs."

I laughed. She had no idea what I was laughing at.

We got off to a side that was covered. We sat on the rail and I lit the last cigarette I had from the party in Wan Chai. It was more poetic this way. Night. Hollowness was helping the tourists by taking pictures of them.

"I am going to miss this place."

"Don't miss me too much. I know it is hard," she said moving her legs back and forth.

"You say that to all the guys you meet, don't you?"

We laughed.

"Look, see? There is the Bank of China. Do you like the light show?" she said pointing somewhere in the distance at the beautifully drawn cardboard of Hong Kong Island.

"What is it with you and Bank of China? Did you work there?"

"No, I just like the way it looks. Those sticks made of light make me feel safe, like everything is okay."

"Shall we get going?"

I threw the cigarette butt in the water. It was polluted anyway. We took the train back holding hands, picked up the suitcase in Fei-yan's room, then took the ride to the airport. We didn't have to wait too long for the bus to pick us up. It was a double-decker, so we took the first row of the upper deck. Hollowness was sitting somewhere in the back.

"You are leaving," Fei-yan said.

"I am."

She took my hand.

At the airport, I checked in and still had some twenty to twenty-five minutes to go. Hollowness was reading a magazine on a chair in the waiting room. From our bench, we could see two gates with security guards where people lined up for passport control.

"What if any of this hadn't happened?"

"This is it, Fei-yan. Our last minutes. Are you ready?"

She started crying. Slow, steady tears down her cheeks.

"You know, Fei-yan, some people are prettier when they smile or laugh. Or maybe their sadness makes them beautiful. But few people are beautiful when they cry. You're one of them."

She laughed and wiped her tears.

"Why are you crying?"

"I think it is obvious. Why do you always have to ask questions? They never do any good."

"Sorry."

"Will I see you again?"

"I'm not sure."

"Will you write to me?"

"Yes, a couple of times."

"Every two weeks."

"It depends."

"Why are you so mean to me right now?"

"I thought things through, Fei-yan. That's all."

"I liked you better when you were drunk. You had hope then. You do not care about me. Why do you have to think things every time? You cannot think these kinds of things. You are mean."

"I'm sorry. But that doesn't mean I don't want to see you again. Things change in ways you can't even see. And it's going to be a long time before we'll see each other. Loving someone is easy, even when you don't say it, but you cry anyway. It's the forgetting part that is long. I read that once in a poem. But everyone it seems, has somewhere to go. We *almost* shared a love story."

She nodded.

"I don't want to leave."

"Do not leave! We can go back to my room, you can stay in my bed, we can figure something out. Do not go."

I thought of going.

"Some things are better left the way there are. And who knows, maybe in the long-run, maybe if I stayed with you right now, you would've turned into another Carina."

"You are hurting me so much, you cannot imagine."

"Do you think it's easy for me? Do you think I'll just walk through that door over there and be over with it? If there is a guy out there who writes our story, then pray to him he's going to write a part where we'll meet again."

"I will. What's his name? How do I find him? Where does he live? Can I write to him?"

"You'll just have to wait. I'll send you what I know in a letter."

I stood up. I put my hand out to Fei-yan.

She wiped her tears again.

"You knew it would come to this."

"Yes."

"Why did you do it, then?"

We paused for another moment in front of the security check.

"It was nice sharing this with you."

I put out my arm again for a handshake. She laughed among her tears and hugged me.

"Bye."

Hollowness stood up from the chair and was waiting for me to go through security.

I looked at it and said, "Stay here. I don't need you anymore."

Hollowness tugged my arm and shirt, mumbling.

"No. Stay. Get away from me."

Hollowness pulled my arm so badly, I thought it was going to break. Hollowness was angry and was snorting, growling, drooling all over my hand, pulling me over to the gate.

"There's nothing you can do now. Go with her. Fei-yan needs you now."

Hollowness gave me a sad look, but in the end stopped behaving like a child. She was unsure what came next. All of us were. Fei-yan could see Hollowness coming to greet her and I stood in her way. As she was fading away in my eyes, Fei-yan seemed to know Hollowness from somewhere. She smiled and reached out her arm.

"Come, he is going to miss his plane if we stay too long. He has to go through security now."

I saw Hollowness – who now looked like a distant relative

of mine – holding hands with Fei-yan. Both of them were waving to me. I lined up for the security check. They didn't want to miss the bus back home, so they walked into the vast night (vaster without her) still holding hands. They never looked back once.

I couldn't believe I was leaving. This must be some sort of joke, because I couldn't feel anything. Fei-yan was supposed to be with me. She'd just gone to the bathroom and should be back any moment now. The guards were urging me to catch my plane, and called for one of those golf carts, because it was the last call; but for me, time expanded. "Hurry up please its time, hurry up please its time," they repeated mechanically. I didn't want to be stuck in an airport, a zone that belongs to nobody in the end. If I could have turned around right now, I would still see Fei-yan coming close to the automatic doors. The guards' arms were reaching for the collar of my shirt and bag. It was a day, just like any other. They had finally heard my prayers.

Hong Kong – Amsterdam 2014

ADVANCE RESPONSES

It is rare for a debut novel, or any novel, to get the macro and the micro right at the same time, but Dragoş Ilca, who writes like the artistic love child of Kafka and Machado de Assis, is already master of both staging the events that make you understand his characters and inventing the bracingly odd images that make you feel them.

HK Hollow is a love story for the Orchid Generation, in which a shared sense of alienation and philoxenia, privilege and deprivation, melancholy and optimism, allows the lovers to bridge the language and luggage that conspire to keep them apart.

—Jonathan Gilll, University of Amsterdam, Author of *Harlem: The Capital of Black America.*

Dragoş Ilca writes with both the innocence of the tourist discovering a new world everyday & also with the passion of an addict. He practices his virtuosity in *HK Hollow* inventing unusual situations, curious scenes and altogether original metaphors. Even though the general vibe of the book is calm and domestic, the core foregrounds a deep and unsettling state.

— Vlad A. Gheorghiu, author and translator

FIND OUT MORE ABOUT PROVERSE AUTHORS BOOKS, LITERARY PRIZES, AND EVENTS

Visit our website:
http://www.proversepublishing.com
Visit our distributor's website: <www.chineseupress.com>

Follow us on Twitter
Follow news and conversation: <twitter.com/Proversebooks>
OR
Copy and paste the following to your browser window and follow the instructions:
https://twitter.com/#!/ProverseBooks

"Like" us on www.facebook.com/ProversePress
Request our free E-Newsletter
Send your request to info@proversepublishing.com.

Availability
Most books are available in Hong Kong and world-wide
from our Hong Kong based Distributor,
The Chinese University Press of Hong Kong,
The Chinese University of Hong Kong, Shatin, NT,
Hong Kong SAR, China.
Email: cup-bus@cuhk.edu.hk
Website: <www.chineseupress.com>.

All titles are available from Proverse Hong Kong
http://www.proversepublishing.com
and the Proverse Hong Kong UK-based Distributor.

We have **stock-holding retailers** in Hong Kong,
Singapore (Select Books),
Canada (Elizabeth Campbell Books),
Andorra (Llibreria La Puça, La Llibreria).
Orders can be made from bookshops in the UK and elsewhere.

Ebooks
Most of our titles are available also as Ebooks.

www.ingramcontent.com/pod-product-compliance
Lightning Source LLC
Chambersburg PA
CBHW051343020726
47501CB00007B/2246